# ORIGIN UNKNOWN

Other Works by Oliver Rohe Available in English Translation

*Vacant Lot*

# ORIGIN UNKNOWN

OLIVER ROHE

TRANSLATED BY LAUREN MESSINA
EDITED BY JANE KUNTZ

DALKEY ARCHIVE PRESS
CHAMPAIGN / LONDON / DUBLIN

Originally published in French as *Défaut d'origine*
by Editions Allia, Paris, 2003



First edition, 2013


Library of Congress Cataloging-in-Publication Data

Rohe, Oliver.
[Défaut d'origine. English]
Origin unknown / Oliver Rohe ; Translated by Lauren Messina ; Edited by Jane Kuntz. -- First Edition.
pages cm
Originally published in French as *Defaut d'origine* by Editions Allia, Paris, 2003.
ISBN 978-1-56478-884-9 (pbk. : alk. paper)
I. Title.
PQ2718.O54D413 2013
843'.92--dc23
2013007220

Partially funded by a grant from the Illinois Arts Council, a state agency

Cet ouvrage a bénéficié du soutien des Programmes d'aide à la publication de Culturesfrance/Ministère français des affaires étrangères et européennes

This work, published as part of a program of aid for publication, received support from CulturesFrance and the French Ministry of Foreign Affairs

www.dalkeyarchive.com

Cover: design and composition by Mikhail Iliatov

Printed on permanent/durable acid-free paper

*The artist turns himself into everything he sees and wants to be.*

—Novalis

*A creative mind may say entirely of its own accord what another has already said before. Then again, another may imitate in advance those thoughts that won't occur to a creative mind until later.*

—Karl Kraus

*Repetition belongs to humor and irony.*
—Gilles Deleuze

They've seated me here, but I hate planes. For years I've been telling myself I'd be better off just traveling in my head—it's been the rule, in fact. They've seated me here and no sooner have I settled in than I'm cursing the endless flight ahead. So, why did I break the rule, I wonder? Roman wasn't what I'd call a very close friend, just a guy I would get together with on occasion, who would sometimes confide in me, that's all. Never heard a word from him since my departure. So why take this trip? Roman has been playing dead for ten years now. Ten years of non-existence, as far as I'm concerned. To be honest, for those whole ten years, I refused to even think about anyone from over there. I didn't want to hear anything more about the people or the place. In fact, I got so good at refusing to think about them that it became second nature. After all, nostalgia is a matter of will, which is what I tell myself as I fasten my seat belt: you either want to remember or you don't. For my part, I was deeply committed to forgetting the whole business. Time to wipe the slate clean, as they say. To nip in the bud once and for all anything that could possibly resemble a resurgence (accidental or otherwise) of my past. The moment I detect the stirrings of nostalgia, or whenever I feel myself insidiously giving in to melancholy, I systematically nip it in the bud. No looking back. Since my departure I've consistently crushed the slightest suggestion of *what could have* been, of whatever sort. I have so successfully applied this agenda, it has become so second nature, that almost nothing from that period subsists. "Would you mind switching places with me? So I can see what it looks like down there. This is my first time on a plane." It's very simple: in my head, it's as if none of it ever happened. For that matter, back when we were still hanging out together ten years ago, Roman would always say that the past is like some clunky piece of furniture. No way to get rid of it. You can't move it, because it's too heavy, you can't pawn it off on someone else. So, all you can do is ignore it. Now that I recall that encounter, in spite of Roman's sensible advice, I wonder even more why I've decided to go back. It certainly does go against all of my rules. Logically, Roman should be nothing more than a blunted memory, and I should have long since jettisoned anything he might have represented back then. Just like the disgusting city I associate him with, (and always will, no matter what). This place, this travesty of a country, this pestilential cesspool that you consider your homeland will never be more than an endless field of ruins; such was the sententious moralizing at which Roman excelled. The carefree inhabitants of this city don't realize that today's streets where they so love to parade are in reality nothing more than an enormous, smoldering cemetery. People here drive their fancy cars, they come and go, strolling and meddling, one big frolic, but they never imagine that right beneath their feet, scattered all over the place, there are the still decomposing bodies that haven't yet had their last word. You need only scratch the surface, Roman said, to readily observe what is barely concealed: vast stretches of mass graves, corpses piled up like garbage, bodies amputated and emaciated, bodies torn to shreds, literally unrecognizable and shrouded hastily in filthy linens. It's possible that even some relative of one of these unsuspecting inhabitants is rotting away beneath their feet at this very moment without their ever knowing, or wanting to know. I'm almost certain that the dog owners (though there are very few, folks over here being incredibly wary of dogs, preferring to kill them off with shotguns; they don't cure rabies here, they preempt it), have no idea where the bones they treat their pets to actually come from. For years, the inhabitants of this city slaughtered each other without really knowing why (no one really knows), and now they're hugging and backslapping as if *nothing had happened.* "Would you like something to drink? A club soda, perhaps?" For more than a decade and a half, all these morons you see everywhere, all these social climbers who are always in your face, this mob of louses dripping with self-importance, were not so long ago, yesterday to be precise, fighting to the death. Blood brothers, next door neighbors or longtime friends were mobilized into separate camps, armed to the teeth, and then ordered to butcher each other blindly, without ever asking why. One day they would be sending each other truce offers, the next, several tons of heavy shells. One day they were signing peace treaties in grand Geneva hotels, the next they were hatching barbaric plots, and on it went, in a spiral of death. None of the protagonists of this sumptuous butchery (or anyone else, now that I think of it), questioned their own motivations, said Roman; we walked lightheartedly towards death, sometimes out of fear of being killed, often out of simple bloodlust. "Could I have your pack of salted peanuts?" Unlike all of history's preceding wars, this one was unencumbered by any pretense of ideological varnish, or any nebulous rhetoric, said Roman; it appealed (though feebly) to our supposed patriotic and communitarian instincts and our no less ostensible predisposition to demagoguery. No need to resort to all that, to all these systems and references, to all these clearly superfluous myths. "Appreciate it, thanks." It was, simply put, a bloody free-for-all, an open-air slaughterhouse, that we would regularly visit, like some family outing, you might say, to stretch our legs. In the end, I even think we entered into the war only out of boredom; we got into it just for something to do, to see what would happen, to *break the monotony of our everyday lives*. If you really think about what actually happened, with enough distance I mean, you will see that none of this made any sense whatsoever, or even the slightest *semblance* of sense. No use spinning grand excuses or convoluted rhetoric, said Roman between sips of coffee; gangs of guys bored out of their minds got together, and there you had it. They armed themselves to the teeth, at first to defend against the *enemy of the moment*, they told us, then to spread major disorder and terror. No one knew *who was pulling the strings*. We watched people arrive on the scene and then we watched these same people beat the daylights out of us. At first they came to defend us and to maintain a little law and order, but once they had accomplished that noble task (the transition was subtle enough, so that no one could truly distinguish between these two phases), once they had gained everyone's trust, they then proceeded quite naturally to commit wanton acts of violence. Get out while you can, we'll protect your property, they told us, and once we'd fled, they grabbed everything we owned. Whenever they coveted a building or an apartment, whenever some fancy house would catch their eye, they would wreak havoc in the neighborhood to spark fear, to make us literally *die of fear* (in their defense, I must admit they also made us die of fear gratuitously and with no hidden agenda, like the day I was forced—gun to my head—to play Russian roulette in the company of the most brainless brute of the neighborhood, pretty obvious that they didn't want our apartment or anything in it, no, what I concluded that day was that, more generally, they could make us die of fear, but just for laughs—all's fair in love and war, as the saying goes. But now when I think back on it, at some point the fear of dying gradually vanishes, you get used to the death threats, which you face with something like the frivolity of youth, we were even capable of playing cards a few meters from a Katyucha rocket launcher, and after a time, the fear of dying had so conditioned us, we had assimilated and internalized it so seamlessly that we had become its docile pets, numb and harmless, and in time, we had so completely shed all fear of danger as to lose not only our dignity but our knack for dying—our humanity). And guys like that, of that particularly despicable, barbaric ilk, we knew them by the dozen. We bred them in our families; we enlisted them into the ranks of those assumed to be our most trusted friends. Guys who would invite themselves to dinner at your house every night for five or six years, guys who, one day, you made the mistake of trusting, and were then the first to stab you in the back. They turn up one day in your absence (some would do so in your presence), park their van at the entrance to your building, and proceed to empty your living room of all of its furniture, rugs, and encyclopedias. These are the ones, these nameless nobodies suddenly endowed with power beyond their wildest dreams; it is these that we have gloriously, though somewhat ingratiatingly, named the warlords. It was with these, the lords of war recruited from among our lowliest scum, that we were able to engage a kind of total, pervasive war, gratuitous, ideology-free war, in a word, a perfectly *modern* war, as Roman (and now I) sums it up. With a war as modern as ours, we didn't need to claw our way up, to bend over backwards, to sell out or whore around, in short, to scale the rungs of a political party in order to win and take all. A war as modern as ours, Roman said that day, gave birth to what could be considered the most democratic political system the world has ever known. Even in their most brazen estimations, in their most ecstatic fever dreams, the true believers of the Communist system would never have dared to envision such prodigious social mobility. The lowliest nonentities, for example, were enthroned in the loftiest chairs of the social hierarchy without first joining the ranks of any sectarian group or armed faction. One day we saw them begging for a penny, and the next, the very next day, they were driving a Mercedes, the kind of revenge typical of the vilest dregs of humanity. Naturally, this unlikely system of upward mobility gave birth to an entire spontaneous generation of sleazes, thugs, and social climbers, so we might as well face the fact, there's no sense hiding it, that we are *nothing but a civilization of social climbers, or to be exact, criminal social climbers.* Our war has turned out to be the laboratory for every war to come, which makes us the first cuddly little samples of an incubating race, a blindly criminal humanity that we can expect to fully mature in a mere thirty to forty years. "That stewardess is a sweetie, isn't she!" An upstart criminal, it's a well-known fact, said Roman, that kind of punk criminal claims all sorts of prerogatives, among them the right of life or death over pretty much everyone, like some feudal lord. The right of life or death all the more liberalized in that our lord of the manor has no notion of scale when it comes to penalties. For wearing his hair long, a young twenty-something man might be shot, execution style, in the back of the head. As for day to day business, the pragmatic matters, as we call them, a warlord or a criminal social climber or a feudal lord—call him what you will—is served ahead of everyone else at the bakery, the gas station, or the supermarket, though it seems somehow obscene to call such stores "super" in a time of acute shortages. "Would you mind if I lowered the blind?" You could stand in line for hours, risking your life, since a 240-kilo bomb could drop on you at any moment, just to buy a little bread or milk or water, when here comes one of the warlord's henchmen to butt in front of you and swipe your bread (once served, they have been known to blow up the bakery with a car bomb). Say for instance that an apartment, your parents' apartment, let's suppose, was considered far too large for four or five occupants; in the best-case scenario, the new bullies of the neighborhood would seize half of it, and in the worst (meaning the most likely scenario), the whole thing. They would follow a kid in the street, wait until the kid opens the door to his building, then they'd knock him out with a rifle butt and kick everyone out of the apartment. Didn't take a genius to think of it. They'd welcome themselves into homes after breaking down the doors with axes, they'd line the whole family up against a wall, beat up or kill the husband depending on the mood of the moment, they'd force the wife to dance half-naked to a frenzied beat, and then leave, laughing hysterically. The list of cases like this goes on forever, every day we'd hear another horrific story, each more horrifying than the last. And always more humiliating. *They humiliated us to death*, that's the bottom line, said Roman, once we were as consistently humiliated as we had been for years on end, once we'd learned to *accept* daily humiliation without batting an eye, once all of our activities, aspirations, our entire lives no longer involved anything beyond our immediate physical survival, we could reasonably conclude, wouldn't you say, that we had been mortally humiliated and that we were consequently mortally disassociated from the rest of humanity. "I borrowed your blanket, I hope you don't mind." People barely had the time to declare their allegiance to the local warlord, to *get used to him*, no sooner had they lovingly submitted, and started to flourish in their servitude, than a brand new petty kinglet, more thuggish than the first, would move in and take over—a highly perfected rotation system that churned out warlords by the thousands. Ultimately, everyone envisioned himself one day or another in the shoes of a warlord, or clearly benefited from the advantageous status: all you needed was a firearm, a somewhat higher than average nasty streak, and enough guts. Naturally, said Roman while putting out his cigarette, naturally, only the most reckless of idiots were that gutsy. A brave person, the kind who would defend a stranger or an old lady in the street, a brave person doesn't value his own life or anybody else's. A brave person, who I insist is the very model of the nasty brute with a heart of gold, is motivated by a disastrously prosaic sense of justice. Even the stupidest of animals can recognize danger, but the brave, the gutsy, those tragically famous everyday heroes, no. The brave are the most basely malleable of all human beings, and it should be obvious that, thanks to battalions of these brave fools, the most heinous crimes in the history of humanity were perpetrated. "Could you turn off the light? It's right in my eyes, I can't sleep with it on." Now that it's all supposedly over (though it is not over, nor will it ever be), and everything is supposedly back to normal, now that everyone is sated, that everyone is exhausted from those long months of slaughter-fest, we're going to have to start thinking about calculating the death toll, about settling the bill, so to speak. Except that no one, especially not the current government, aka, yesterday's most bullish killers, seriously intends to settle much of anything. Roman figured (as did I) that after so many years, there remained not a single innocent victim, no more boundaries, moral ones at least, between the executioners and their victims. He figured that the poor innocents we so readily deplore would have acted like ruthless executioners themselves, given the slightest chance (and many did, in fact), that these loathsome victims, it turns out, should have defended themselves like everyone else did (and they had every opportunity). Today, we simply no longer have the wherewithal to save anyone, and even less to lie to ourselves. Everyone was so keen to share in the crime, so everyone should have to pay. And yet, in a country so fanatically in love with its own sordidness, said Roman, in a country where abjection and ignorance literally comprise the unsurpassable intellectual and moral standard, in a country where crime and denial of crime are considered a necessary form of social hygiene, no one will ever pay. As I leave my seat, immediately taken over by my neighbor, (whose name I don't remember, even though he warmly introduced himself only fifteen minutes ago), I wonder how these more or less normal people, people who don't seem in any way impaired, how these people can close their eyes, let alone sleep, suspended in the void. They probably don't realize how dangerous it is, they consider flying to be something perfectly normal. They must be either very brave or very oblivious (I now believe these two terms to be one and the same). I must confess that the more I think about Roman, the worse I feel, *the more his monologues stream through my brain, the less I hear my own voice,* and the more I look into the aircraft's tiny bathroom mirror, the more I perceive almost in focus, his angular face peering over my shoulder. Yet nothing he has said, nothing he could ever say, has contradicted my own analyses or my own opinions, whatever they may be. Ever since he's gone incommunicado, (and I did nothing to stop him from doing so), I've resolved to no longer let his words infiltrate my thoughts, and while I'm at it, I've made the very wise decision to disavow that entire part of my existence. I've convinced myself that a fresh start would require a small dose of amnesia, that selecting one part of one's memories at the expense of another, that mixing the old with the new, in short, attempting to outsmart one's own memory, would always, irreversibly and disastrously, lead to an uncontrollable flood of nostalgia. Roman embodied everything I had wanted to systematically destroy for the last ten years, I thought as I made my way back to my seat, but we are incapable, pathetically incapable of sticking to a resolution. In fact, we're so perverse and inconsistent that we've managed to convince ourselves that the whole thing, this neat little exercise in self-destruction, was *for the best,* for our *own good.* That this resolution I myself aborted was perhaps not that appropriate. That perhaps it should never have been made in the first place. That it should never have been left to germinate in my mind. How many plans laid with determination, enthusiasm, and excitement have quickly fallen through under my very own complicit, thankful gaze, and how many times have I then resorted to perversely miraculous expedients? "The Captain wishes to inform you that we will soon be entering a zone of strong turbulence, please fasten your seatbelts." Looked at more closely, even willpower is an unfounded projection, in a way. It doesn't matter that you have the will to achieve this or that grand goal, for example, to very carefully and completely suppress an entire slice of your life; sure, you can convince yourself of a bunch of other things that are presumably achievable, but just a hint of lucidness brings you back to earth. I have seen enough to know that willpower is useless, except as temporary relief, meaning that we get to lie to ourselves a little longer. You say to yourself, what if I did this or that, and then, of course, you don't do it; you never do it. We abhor anything challenging, so we bend and give in; and stop at nothing to justify our deficiencies. We abhor anything challenging, and what's worse, we know how pathetic everything is, how even our most remarkable achievements only signify dismal defeat. And the more we realize that nothing lasts, that everything inevitably leads to nothing, that all our so-called exploits lead nowhere but the grave, we get discouraged, and end up not believing in our own little mind games, so we give up and die away. What's at work behind all these wicked lies we inflict on ourselves is the will. "This is the first time I've been on an airplane, and I'm actually not afraid of all of this turbulence." In this fucking country there has never been anything but war and money and now oblivion and money, Roman was forever repeating back when I used to run into him in one of those flashy downtown bars, *in this fucking country there has never been anything but war and money, and now oblivion and money, or, to paraphrase an obscure Prussian corporal, the continuation of war by other means.* For years, mass murder was allowed to prosper, and we encouraged the proliferation of armed vermin for years on end, we organized wholesale butchery, for more than fifteen years, to be exact, we did everything so that murder found in *all of us* the most worthy representatives and now, now that it's time to get serious about paying for this unprecedented genocidal rodeo, we're told to forget everything, to wipe the slate clean, as they put it. They tell us it's time to start all over and to *reset the clock*. In other words, it's time to delete the memories, that's the simple truth. The nerve of this new war is memory, said Roman. To win, we're going to delete our memories, they said. Erase everything. Erase everything immediately and from day one, and *without missing a beat.* Nothing should remain in your mind. Blank pages. Your mind reduced to blank pages without missing a beat, they basically tell us. No evidence, not a fragment, not a trace, nothing of what *actually took place* must resist our plunge into collective amnesia. Nothing. Act as if *nothing had ever happened*, and that's an order. Blank pages, your minds are blank pages, they tell us. They wrecked everything, and amassed the ruins, they spared literally nothing, and now they want all that erased, immediately and from day one. They forced twenty percent of the population into exile, while the corpses continued to pile up in this extermination frenzy and now, said Roman, now, consistent with their own logic, *they continue the carnage, but softly*. Killing us softly with oblivion. With blank pages. Forever rehashing and re-rehashing the same events, the same hardships, the same pain, there's something obscene about that, isn't there, they claim, and in such bad taste. Better to just reset the clock. And don't miss a beat, right? Get rid of those memories right now. And from this day forward, may all your unjustified nightmares promptly change into dreams of across-the-board reconciliation. *You saw nothing, experienced nothing: it's all in your head.* Effective immediately, you will swallow the fairy tale that we've served up for you, no questions asked. You have lost neither son nor daughter, brother or sister or wife or home or anything at all: it's all in your head. Move along, we'll handle the pardons. It's all in your head, but we'll pardon anyway. Besides, nothing happened at all, from the very start, *you have simply been dreaming.* Anyway, nobody is guilty, there will be no breast-beating or mourning, no purges, they tell us. There will be none of these things because nothing ever really happened, of course not, since we committed nothing and consequently, we aren't responsible for anything. And to prove to you that we are categorically not responsible for anything, we will forthwith entrust ourselves with the responsibility of the country. To prove our innocence, we simply entrust ourselves with the responsibility of the country, they assured us. And without missing a beat, said Roman, the collective evidence of their innocence couldn't wait and so they didn't wait. It was *quite literally overnight* that our most illustrious warlords were cleared of their innumerable crimes, said Roman, scot-free, so to speak, no questions asked, and without pulling the Go To Jail card, they traded their old blood-smeared fatigues for the respectable three-piece suit of the minister, literally overnight. Monday they left up to their elbows in gore and Tuesday they were back, all tricked out as cabinet ministers. War criminals and ministers get along so well together, Roman said as he lit a cigarette, they coexist so harmoniously in the same body that there's no way to tell them apart. One and the same. *It's the same guys all over again and the crime never happened.* "Would you like the fish or the chicken?" And of course, said Roman that day, of course these are the same criminals whitewashed into ministers who are working to obliterate the memories, they're the ones—along with almost everyone else, mind you—who drone on the loudest about how it's time to reset the clocks, and pronto. We want more than ever, they tell us, we want more than ever to reset the clocks and *move forward together, hand in hand, into the future.* Blank pages and without missing a beat. Ever since we assumed responsibility of running the country we have never known happier times, they tell us, so don't worry about anything: just forge ahead, everyone together, en masse. Enthusiasm is what we need today, enthusiasm and a can-do attitude, we have to stick together, and store up all the good will we can, and channel all our energy toward a single goal: moving forward. Not a single voice should stand out or say no, or rise above the others, since the real criminals, we are told, the real criminals are those who aren't enthusiastic enough about this fairy-tale future that we're preparing for them. Stopping to question things, or even to think, would be tantamount to a crime against history on the march, so says the official discourse, an unforgivable heresy—punishable offenses. Resist even momentarily this genuine *terror by enthusiasm* and you'll be charged as a heretic, the designated enemy of recovery. Memory is now analogous to a crime against recovery, said Roman, and anyone who dares preserve a few memories of what actually took place will get the appropriate treatment: the stake. "I'll bring you that right away." Everything we destroyed, everything *you* destroyed must be rebuilt immediately, they tell us. We must show the whole world—and the eyes of the world are upon us, aren't they—that we have not backed down, that we all fervently desire, in one common yearning, as one man, to forget everything and rebuild everything. The world has got to know that we will erase every bit of rubble and every scar of the war that we aren't responsible for. (Roman told me one evening as we walked amidst the ruins of the city center, which at the time still abounded in impassable streets and gutted buildings, he told me that in order to truly purge our minds of this war, we must purge the architecture of anything that might remind us. This headlong rush to rebuild is really nothing but the architectural facet of the grand memory-evacuation operation, he said.) Proud, yes, we are proud to forget everything and to rebuild from the ground up, they tell us. But we are equally proud of what we are, our past and our traditions. Our history, our roots, our traditions, we are the envy of the whole world; our *festival feeling*, our legendary hospitality, our amazing business sense, our aptitude for languages, all of this and more must be carefully preserved. We will not betray our land, our ancestors, or our *identity.* But beware, they hasten to add, let's not get stuck in the past: confident in our *identity*, we shall envision the future with serenity and erase everything from this moment on. Preserving the inconvenient after-effects of those nasty few years is simply not an option, we must rebuild everything and without further delay. *Our country, our cities, and our hinterlands are now declared a national project and we need the whole world watching us to know that we are one huge national project.* Without further delay we shall turn everything into a project and build—*on the very scenes of the crime,* said Roman—palaces, shopping malls, casinos and buildings of prodigious excess. Everything must be rebuilt immediately and extravagantly, the *glitzier* the better. We will stop at nothing, however underhanded, to restore our credibility in the eyes of the world, no skimping, whatever it takes, they tell us, to entice the visiting businessmen and even artists, for that matter. The visiting businessmen and, for that matter, the artists, no longer need to stay away; this is the so-called recovery they're concocting for us. Palaces, above all else, palaces, golf courses, casinos, and spas and you'll see tourists coming back in droves. For too long, tourists have shunned us, and too long have we turned our backs on them; to put it bluntly, we fucked up, so we've got some serious catching up to do. With extravagance and glitz. Decimated but proud, that's how these people are, said Roman, decimated but proud of our pimping and hustling (for those are the applicable terms) for new tourists. How will we dazzle them? We'll start by throwing money at the biggest names in fashion, business, and industry, or so they tell us. As long as we're still standing, they claim, as long as we're still kicking, we will always know which way the winds of fashion are blowing. Our country, our beautiful country has always been terribly fashion-conscious, a whimsical side that we're more than a little proud of, our country has always prided itself in being well-dressed and must remain so, it's generally agreed, including among the underclass. We're ready to import the highest of high-end products so as to always remain ahead of the curve, when it comes to fancy brands and glitz, even if it means starving (I knew a number of people who were starving underneath their designer clothes, or living twelve to a room in slums while driving a Mercedes, a rather peculiar yet widespread notion of dignity). People slept five to a shelter beneath a shower of mortar shells, but their shelter was often the leather interior of luxury sedans. We didn't have enough water, bread and milk; we were, as they say, brutally reduced to a prehistoric animal-like state, but never to the point of neglecting our dress, hairstyles, or nail polish. I remember that after two nearly uninterrupted weeks in a shelter, survival wasn't nearly as important as displaying the most luxurious, spacious, and flashy car possible, Roman mused, so that after two to three weeks of intense one-upmanship, you could no longer see anything but luxury cars at our shelter, or at the very least, cars designed for the highest possible comfort given the circumstances. Even in the darkest hours of our history, they told us, even when the world was unjustly turned away, we managed to stay well-dressed and high-spirited underneath the roofs of our sedans—in short, we kept our dignity intact. We managed, however horrendous the circumstances, to spare no expense and to save face. So rest assured, they told us, as long as we're in charge, we won't relent in this ongoing struggle to save face—a tradition that has earned us the admiration of nations. Maybe we're the asshole of the world, but an *asshole that is always impeccably dressed,* I'll grant them that, said Roman (and I granted them the same). "Can I take your meal tray?" Not only an always impeccably dressed asshole, but one that strives to hustle, seduce and fling open the doors to a host of internationally respected artists, said Roman. Complete recovery also depends on art and culture, something they like to say in their official speeches. With the approach of summer, Roman used to always say that the country would dive head first into a collective artistic trance that would take everyone months of rest to recover from. To regain some semblance of civilization, we must reconcile with art, they tell us, we must renew our connection to internationally respected performers. *We have long developed a close relationship with great world performers, and it's high time they came back to sing on our stages.* We must not only encourage them to return to our stages to sing (to the tune of millions, by the way) but we need to secure the loyalty of as many of them as possible. In this country, a world-class performer must still be able to feel at home, they tell us; we must show them that our legendary sense of hospitality remains perfectly intact. They have fulfilled this mission so well that today the country is positively awash in internationally respected performers. In summer, you're quite likely to cross paths with famous faces just about everywhere, on beaches, in nightclubs or restaurants, marveled Roman; some of these celebrities even feel so at home that they've started taking up residence here. You can only imagine (I had a hard time imagining myself) how desperate an internationally respected performer had to be to decide to settle here, in this asshole of the world—a well-dressed one, granted, but certainly not worthy of their world-class talent. *At the same time that this huge national-scale construction site was being set up, the country was also becoming an enormous, non-stop cultural festival* where the greatest voices on the planet, the most famous musicians of Europe, and the most respected international performers came to perform, one after the other; we even recently had the indescribable honor (an enduring honor, it should be said) of receiving world-renowned fashion models. All of these people, all these great performers, intellectuals, and other icons of fashion who gratify us with their presence, participate, perhaps unwittingly, in recovering our credibility with the international community, some might well think. When the world has actually seen the effect of what we've been nurturing—again, to the tune of millions—the biggest internationally renowned performers, they tell us, when the world sees how much we love these performers, how much we are *truly* performers at heart ourselves, well, that world can no longer ignore or scoff at us: and this is the brilliant scheme they hope the world will fall for. "Would you like tea or coffee?" Of course, here again, there will be consequences down the line, and someone will eventually have to pay. Mingling so closely with art and cultivating such strong ties to high art circles doesn't come without consequences, Roman reiterated, which is why today we are witnessing the breeding of an entire *spontaneous generation* of tormented, sublimely pathetic artists (I know a good number of them). We had war and money, war and oblivion, we hoarded so much catastrophe, so to speak, that now we have a natural right to spawn an *obscene* number of artistic sensibilities. In every family, in every corner of every café, in every circle of friends today there abounds the sensitive artist, the sensitive poet, the sensitive philosopher or sensitive musician, it seems that this whole country is suffering from a disgustingly prodigious artistic glut. Through our own fault, or rather, the fault of our parents, we have thus created a sublime new race of uppity artists. All of these years of systematic demolition could obviously not go unpunished and our punishment today, undoubtedly the most sinister, certainly the most painful to endure, is to foster among us, in our own homes and among our near and dear, the spawning of so many sublimely uppity artistic sensibilities. And to complete the picture, pursued Roman, a bunch of ridiculous posers playing the wounded artist (is there any such thing as a wounded artist, really?) that in fact are only mimicking the artist's lifestyle, that is a lifestyle *rooted in idleness and gossip.* There's a kind of rampant inspiration inflation going on in this country, where even your garden variety teen has a direct line to the muses or claims some special artistic bent; in reality, the most pretentious have claimed they receive artistic inspiration as if by divine fiat for which they are but the humble vector. We are only instruments in the service of genius, they say with a perfectly straight face. You get the impression that everyone is tuned into the same vibe, the whole country is somehow thunderstruck by high art, that it has even transformed into one gigantic workshop of continuous creation. The proliferation of artistic rabble (and it is rabble, how else can you describe it) is such that it is now almost impossible to step out your front door day or night without bumping into some self-important, sublimely puffed up artist type. Go to any café and you'll hear poetry slams, visit friends and you'll have to put up with their posing, start any discussion and all you'll get back is rhymes and aphorisms. In fact, the aphoristic form has itself become the basic structure of language, said Roman, and in certain circles, the most abysmal of course, people speak in nothing but aphorisms, maxims, and other pearls of wisdom. What is so absolutely unbearable about this aphoristic drift is the sort of inane Nietzsche cult that has gripped the country; everyone here has read him (often at one go, say the braver souls) or thinks they've read him; not a moron around who doesn't claim to *identify* with the—and I quote—"biting" aphorisms of the German master, there is not one who doesn't insinuate offhandedly, as if it had just occurred to him, that Nietzsche says out loud what he, the sublime artist, had been thinking to himself for a long time, nor is there a moron that hesitates pointing out *how much he personally owes to* Nietzsche—to the point where poor Nietzsche has been basically elevated, or reduced to, the role of the chief creditor of the nation. It also happens that the most idiotic, meaning those who have supposedly penetrated the maze of great Nietzschean thought, claim with a kind of pompous sincerity whose absurdity clearly escapes them, that to take on the philosophy of Nietzsche is to take on an immense danger, that losing themselves in the *soul-stirring incantations* of the genius from Sils Maria—they do like to vary their names for him—amounts to accepting the inevitability of an irreversible nervous collapse. And what's even more repugnant in this unhealthy affection for the well-placed, heartfelt aphorism, is the systematic reference to the unreadable Cioran and his abysmal essay *The Trouble with Being Born* every other sentence. Cioran got it right, they say: we didn't ask to be born, we are all desperately unhappy, despair is our most *basic feeling;* we are simply not designed for happiness. *Cioran got it right because he too was unhappy*, they repeat, and it's this unhappiness—note the equivalence of concepts—that makes us so hopeless. Now all they need is to add Celine to the mix, and to start using ellipses everywhere to completely annihilate us. "A hot towel, sir?" As soon as he picked up on snippets of conversation at the table next to us, Roman said, he found conclusive proof of everything he'd just been talking about. All I need to corroborate my hypothesis is right here, said Roman; just listen carefully to what those guys behind us are saying, and you'll realize that art today is martyred, exploited, and even held hostage (and will always be, I'm fairly certain) by this entire tribe of sublimely sensitive artists. In this country, more than any other, we confuse art and suffering, art and life's miseries, art and troubles. There isn't a single one of these kids that doesn't justify his artistic pretensions by the experience of war, but they all flatten it into nothing but a form of therapy. And this is the tragedy, said Roman. I need to write, they say, voice quivering; I can't live without writing or painting, they also say while removing their gloves; writing or painting is as natural for me as breathing, they say finally while scratching their forearms; this is the rhetoric, the typical scene as staged today. And yet, we all know, don't we, that as soon as we hear young people, wherever they're from, talking about literature or painting or music in terms of need—not in terms of *simulation* and *artifice*, but in terms of need—more generally as soon as we hear that these same young people are stamping their need to paint or write with the seal of necessity, you can be pretty sure you're dealing with a bunch of mannered morons. Young guys like that awful Gabriel that you met last night, remember him, that sentimental, fragile thing that composes poems on the rape of innocence (I vaguely remember him), guys like that bore you to tears, we're breeding them by the thousands these days, indeed this whole supposedly hypersensitive generation whose need to write or paint is matched only by their lack of talent, well, they make up more than half of today's youth. So Gabriel is hardly an exception, all of these punks are either fully formed Gabriels or budding Gabriels. Note that everyone here discovered his *Gabriellian* artistic sensibility *after* the war, and there is not one who fails to write or rhyme or compose with the rape of innocence as the main topic. Yet dealing Gabriel-style, meaning just as deeply, with a theme as serious or supposedly serious, Roman said, is enough to give you the shakes, violent diarrhea or severe incurable diseases—at least this is the kind of affliction that they *wish* they suffered from, Gabriel-style (more than the so-called curse of the so-called tortured poet, it's the preferably chronic ailment, like asthma, that provides literature with its most grotesque clichés, and it is probably thanks to Nietzsche that the most incapable artists see in disease, whether real, imagined or aspired to, a precondition, or worse, a synonym for genius, Roman would often say). These diseased types like our Gabriel even began to declare themselves avant-garde, to meet regularly in cafés to discuss the *situation of art*, as they say, and ultimately, to begin writing perfectly inept manifestos. Having attended these assemblies from afar, I can tell you with certainty that these idle conversations have absolutely nothing to do with art. How could it be otherwise for that matter, how could art become a topic of conversation, asked Roman; anything that does get talked about in these ridiculous discussions, which always take place at night, as you might expect, can only amount to pedantry. They gather in large apartments, pass the joint around while contemplating the ceiling and endlessly arguing; they next maintain that they are feeling enormous pain, that their situation is intolerable, that they are bored out of their minds. And instead of rushing to the psychiatrist's office, they sprawl all over the blank page, instead of seeking the couch or medicating themselves like everyone else, they begin a new stanza. Naturally, they'll then go on to justify their artistic frigidity, since no one has written or painted or composed anything based on the traumatic experience of war. (At the time when Roman was holding forth here, the inevitable flip side of this superficial artistic effervescence was the driest of artistic deserts.) Everyone blamed their fundamental incapacity to produce anything on this poor war, which they pumped for all it was worth. The war excuses everything, it relieves all guilt and even absorbs all sorts of despicable acts committed in its name; the slightest personal failure, an unfinished poem or an aborted erection, for example, are now all ascribed to the war. We are not responsible for our failures, they say, it's the war and its horrific consequences that drove us off the cliff (if only the West could follow our example and reap all the benefits of a good war, Roman told me on one of our drinking binges; in barely fifty years of peace, Westerners have forgotten everything, even their own interests. They lament and punish themselves, they bear the guilt of the world's slightest failure, and then regroup to naval-gaze. No, really, what the West needs is a good slaughter to get them over their guilt, he concluded). Ultimately, and along the same specious line of reasoning, war serves as both the motor and the brake of artistic creation, and this is the contradiction they so complacently embrace. They want the lifestyle and the status and the so-called noble suffering of the artist, but are loath to pay the price. They push their justifications so far that they eventually find a certain aristocratic elegance in each of their failures, they end up seeking only the romantic aesthetic of failure, the aesthetic of the *beautiful loser*, otherwise known as failure itself. We thus move from abominable artistic posturing to the no less abominable claim of the elegance of failure, but of course none of these kids has any idea of what failure truly means. And the poets who ascribe their motivations and downfall to a single cause—the war, as if I need mention—simply do not meet the definition of artist or even fallen artist, in fact none of these pathetic posers will ever amount to anything and it's this hard truth they're so unwilling to admit. They'll never amount to anything, and these guys are clearly art's worst enemy, Roman dryly concluded. "We will be screening a feature film shortly, and remind you that headphones are available." Everything these years have produced, everything they could produce in the future, said Roman, will never have anything to do with art or refinement or anything even vaguely civilized. We have every reason to expect that, for decades to come, we'll see nothing but violence, the infinite reproduction of violence in identical or possibly enhanced forms. It doesn't take long to get used to the taste of blood; that may sound pompous, but *here is the truth behind that statement,* it doesn't take long to get used to the taste of blood, and so we attempt to recreate this special taste in the way we behave, in our every thought and deed. The urge to kill doesn't go away overnight, said Roman, and while waiting for the war to start again (and it will certainly start again), all these people who have killed each other in such sportsmanlike ways and who made such considerable fortunes during those years, there's no way that all these people will lose their taste for blood overnight. So, they bide their time. Look for new opportunities. Retrain and diversify: by dying in car accidents or on the ski slopes or in brawls, for example. Here are these guys who fought to within an inch of their lives, and instead of being afraid, instead of hiding out for good, they retrained and diversified, and why wouldn't they, after all? They all consider themselves miraculous survivors but they still shoot at each other in nightclubs. Even today, meaning more than five years later, they're still beating the crap out of each other and shooting each other, said Roman; every time they get the chance to shed some blood, they go for it: they retrain and diversify. They don't just seize opportunity, they create it, they're lying in wait for it (I still remember that the verb they affectionately used to define this manner of provoking bloodshed was *to treat*, they would say *let's go treat ourselves to a shootout, treat ourselves to a brawl, or to a battering,* I remember now). Any excuse, a word or look considered hostile or even unpleasant, justified bloodshed. They managed to escape the carnage of war, but in their eyes, a party wasn't a party without a good fistfight, a shootout, or someone getting his skull cracked open with a baseball bat. Their survival was miraculous, granted, but they will stop at nothing to score another death, said Roman. Smash a nose, slash an eye or shoot someone point blank, these are not things that we can afford to miss out on, they say very openly, we simply can't hold ourselves back like that, and anyway, do you think we're fags or something, they say. What it all means, in the end, Roman said, is that narrowly escaping death, escaping what should have happened merely fed their immoderate *taste* for blood: they would have far and away preferred to not have survived, in fact—probably because survival never meant anything except learning to love violence, brutality, or the taste of blood, however shamefully. Obviously, we're trying to forget these unmentionable urges, dumping them into the black holes of our memory, and at times we even madly endeavor to distort the past that gave rise to them in the first place; but of course nothing is forgotten, especially not violence, much less the looming specter of death to come. We strive to erase but fail once more, attempt to flee and we're caught, we try to control ourselves and the *same thing happens all over again*, said Roman. We simply cannot put it behind us, even the tiniest bit of what once was, even what we had blindly entrusted to the restorative effects of passing time, which in fact never really passes, but accompanies us, follows us, hunts us down. "I've already seen this movie, what about you?" Now that I recall this exact conversation, now that the entirety of what was said that day (it was a Tuesday night, if my memory serves), has resurfaced, as they so aptly say, I feel the irrepressible need (I'm still experiencing it at this moment), to not think about it anymore, or to revive anything, or stir anything up, but rather to relentlessly pursue the effort to rebuild everything, to gather my strength to *move forward.* It's perfectly useless, even dangerous, to be forever brooding over things willy-nilly, it's why we've been turning in circles, why we've turned in on ourselves to the point of extinction, ruminating over and over. Move forward, wipe the slate clean, and imagine a new future; in short, rebirth and rebuilding were the most affordable solutions, my most reasonable options from the start, which I've been implementing for over ten years now. You can't remain a prisoner of history forever, it would be absurd and suicidal, you can't be here and there at the same time, in that remote and indecipherable limbo that we call, for convenience's sake, the past. No more than you can cobble together coherent abstractions, sometimes called well-tailored narratives, and just innocently tack them onto our past. The past is basically irrational, inconsistent and illogical, the term itself is somehow overly obliging, artificial and arbitrary by definition. And this past that we *give shape to* (that I never cease to give shape to), these relationships that we try so desperately to fabricate for ourselves are nothing more than pathetic *retrospective fictions*. The past, let's face it, is nothing but a pathetic retrospective fiction. To rehash everything is absurd, artificial, and perilous, forward is most assuredly the way to move. Forget everything, shove it all into oblivion, this is what I've disciplined myself to do. This is the journey I'm on, even though it produces the unexpected consequence of dredging up the past, a journey of questionable relevance that brought on the impromptu rant you've just been listening to here. This is all the more grotesque in that I've always had fear of flying (and still do). "You have to watch this movie, it's hysterical, you really should see it." I even loathe all of the passengers and crew aboard this plane, especially the unspeakable boor who first took over my seat, then my peanuts, then my blanket. How to tell him to shut up and leave me alone, but especially, how to resist the urge to beat the crap out of him. What's the use wrestling with all this, questioning why we do or fail to do things; there is no possible explanation, there never has been. Violence is something we tend either to ignore, or to expediently file under the broader category of our standard clichés, said Roman that same Tuesday, but violence is the only thing that we can seriously associate with death, without affectation or complacency, (violence and death were often delivered together, not a single violent act that I ever witnessed went unaccompanied by death, and not a single death was ever non-violent). Unlike disease, which we naturally associate with a body's inevitable dilapidation, unlike this more or less predictable and pre-determined projection in time, said Roman, violence, whether viewed close up or at a distance, always evokes immediate death, sudden, heartless and brutal death. The worst of our punishments, Roman resumed after a brief moment of absence that I remember very clearly, the worst of our punishments, the kind of excruciating condition that has us forever compromising, is our *situation as witnesses*; as long as we haven't yet witnessed anything, we're still waiting to be born. We could effectively date our birth to the day that we first witnessed something dark, something violent, something literally fatal. As long as we haven't seen anything inhuman, or rather, deeply human, as long as our retina hasn't yet been imprinted with the spectacle of the most absolute and bluntest horror, as long as our retina is still able to look around and see something other than a looming shadow, in that case, we're only titillating the worst from a safe remove—we can only conjure it up in daydreams—of course, always in a much watered down version. It's a well-known fact, said Roman, that the more you're called to witness, the more you mix with horror, the further your retina delves into the world's darkest depths, that forgotten dumping ground of pervasive crime—and that's where you'll find the truth. Now that I'm able to define myself almost exclusively as a witness, death is no longer a source of metaphysical anguish for me, nor is it some kind of seductive philosophical concept; but has instead become something more immediately *tangible.* The death I've witnessed is thus the only certainty I've known, one that is constantly borne out by the facts, and that I accept without complaint. After all, aging is surely not a mere matter of racking up the years, nor does it involve the accumulation of temporal sequences without any apparent connection other than straightforward chronology; rather, it's about building up one's store of testimony, cutting and splitting yourself, slicing through the retina a little more each time, which is why I think of myself as already old, in a way, already dead. I can testify, said Roman, I am almost completely finished and it's become impossible for me today, several years now since the tragedy, to participate in anything at all. I can't participate in anything at all anymore, repeated Roman, I'm doomed to renunciation, and now that I am almost dead, I am finally free—or duty-bound, I'm not sure which—to *list the ghosts*, as they pompously say. Of course, you don't get out unscathed from the cesspool that the war years steeped us in, we've emerged with a totally altered perception of the world and of ourselves, or to put it differently, the war years left us literally *deflowered and atrophied and stained and exhausted*, but most of all, it left us with the bitter taste of years lost. "You're really missing out, I'm telling you." Some are the more affected, the more annihilated by all this, some will never get over it. Probably not the criminals as you might guess, but the terrified witnesses, the terrified witnesses who identify with both criminal and victim, this is what's so abject about our situation as witnesses. The witness doesn't actively participate in anything, said Roman, he just ends up there somehow, so there he is, watching, waiting for it to be over; he's just there, and without acting directly on events, he watches the scene *in its entirety*; the ghoulish burden of impartial and panoramic observation rests on his shoulders: *the witness doesn't side with anyone but potentially identifies with everyone*. What's scariest about this wretched condition as witness isn't tied to the fact that witnesses instinctively identify with the victim, said Roman, sympathy of this sort being utterly normal, nor is it a reflection on our own fear of death, it's none of that, but rather the shameful, monstrous, and appalling identification with the executioner. In a few weeks, you'll have the good fortune of leaving for good, the good fortune never to return, to settle accounts forever with this plague-ridden cesspool that is your so-called country. In a few weeks you'll be rid of all this, of this fucked up country that persists in methodically destroying us at every turn. I'm not so fortunate, said Roman, it's all over for me, I can't be a part of anything anymore: my world is now nothing but ghosts, gloom, and thousands of bodies, nameless and forgotten (Roman often spoke of his hopeless inability to participate in anything, how he seemed to be living in a sort of cage of *indifference* amid the busy world. Not that anything in this world ever escaped him: from his invisible prison cell he had a breathtaking view of reality, as they say. He could see everything, watched and took note; but never to the point of joining in. There will always be, he said, this gap, this filter, this veil of indifference between the world of reality, its events, and me). I advise you to stay over there and to never set foot here again; coming back here, even just on holiday, would be the beginning of the end for you, or the end itself. As soon as you hit the tarmac don't give this place another thought, forget everything you ever saw here. Forget your supposed roots, forget your purported history, forget everything, absolutely everything, even your own language, *especially your own language*, which is to say that *bastardized, squishy and shapeless thing* that you'd be well advised to cast off unflinchingly and in full. This mongrel language is as bastardized as your supposed roots, as bastardized as the people you think you belong to, as bastardized as the whole fucked up country that will always have your worst interests at heart. When I think that this language they're so mindlessly proud of is effectively nothing but a disgracefully empty shell, I conclude that forgetting it is a most basic imperative, that forgetting is a matter of survival. We juggle languages here, we practice languages, we are perfectly capable of properly expressing ourselves when abroad, but here we don't even have our own language, *we're nothing but dabblers, our language is the source of our nonbeing, the origin of our decay.* Everyone here boasts of his fluency in this or that language, they even simulate a natural trilingualism but no one, especially not the better educated, which is to say the biggest fools of them all, is able to thoroughly master his mother tongue, because *this language simply doesn't exist.* Of course, you can't completely erase the damned thing from your brain, you'll probably practice it as a hobby from time to time, you'll mix it with other languages just as you're doing right now, but as long as you don't violently dislodge it from your head, as long as you haven't forgotten it for good, it'll stick with you and link you back to this country, even keeping you from mastering any *idiom* whatsoever. In the end, Roman saw the language as an enormous forgery; he even accused the vile thing of preventing him from thinking properly, of undermining his reasoning process. He would often say that a language so infested with borrowings, so incapable of resisting the snobbery of the local polyglots, doesn't provide the necessary tools for thought formation. You simply cannot think properly with three languages milling about in the brain, he harangued. "You're wrong not to be watching this movie, it's a nice little romantic comedy." Feel absolutely no nostalgia, Roman said to me that day (his recommendations always took on the gravitas of a last will and testament, Roman was always one for solemn declarations), you have to nip in the bud the slightest sense of nostalgia you might be feeling. As soon as a wave of melancholy, even the most benign, even the mildest, washes over you, you've got to nip it in the bud, no looking back. Nostalgia is a matter of will, declared Roman, you either want to remember or you don't. Naturally, you will be inclined to remember, remembering is only normal, you'll even feel that rehashing the past is a way of flexing your identity muscles, and by that I mean a suicidal exercise that will make you believe you're not a nobody from nowhere, that you have more or less identifiable origins, more or less honorable origins that you could reasonably be proud of (actually, there's nothing to be even moderately proud of in these origins, and now that I feel sure that I'm completely detached from my past, I know that such matters as language have nothing to do with pride, quite the opposite, and speaking for myself, I have every reason to be ashamed of my origins, ashamed of everything they don't represent, ashamed of the mindless inertia, of the inevitable perdition and the definitive annihilation that these origins underpin). This whole pointless retrospective journey leads nowhere, and certainly not to some ideal starting point, no definite origin, all of this inner turmoil over nothing, all of these imaginary ties that you might sometimes be tempted to forge with the past, I'm afraid they're nothing more than a gigantic deadly hoax. *Renounce your origins, it's an absolute must, not just renounce but denounce your own origins,* declared Roman, upping the ante a bit, and while you're at it, show your contempt for the sycophants that praise them, since the whole notion of origin exists only to be dislodged, uprooted and combated. "Quick, look, here's my favorite part. You have to see this, it really is a good movie, I'm serious." Once you've crossed the borders, consider yourself rather as a kind of stateless person who delights in not belonging to anything or anyone (that's what I've been trying to think all along), tell yourself that you're better off being a renegade, an ingrate or a determined amnesiac than a sentimental idiot unhinged by the memories of a homeland, than an idiot who unwittingly participates in his own annihilation. More than a natural duty, it's actually an enormous privilege not to belong to anything or anyone, a real blessing, and whenever I see, or read, or hear of all these great exiled writers and intellectuals moaning about losing their roots, Roman noted, a few days before my departure, I don't know whether to laugh in their face or slap them: languishing is what these people do, they're professional languishers. Every time I read one of these writers waxing eloquent over his vanished country, I feel an irrepressible urge to puke, and ever since I began reading, or as the self-important scholars say, ever since I began *engaging* these authors, I have never managed to finish reading a book that evokes the tender memory of an abandoned country, culture, or language (and neither have I). I suspect that even these so-called great writers in exile see their uprooting as a smart career move, a profitable business asset, something like an exotic specialty shop and nothing more—some even voluntarily uproot to get their little business off the ground. These great writers who sing or mourn for their former homeland are flooding the literary market with their exotic products, *this dreadfully sentimental literature, this cravenly mercantile literature,* and that's the truth. These grand wandering pen-pushers have never understood the prison they've made for themselves, said Roman; what they don't know, or pretend not to know, it depends on who you mean, is that what they address, with requisite trembling voice, as their roots, or origins, or mother tongue, is nothing but an invisible prison whose oppression they secretly regret; the way I see it, this whole line of exiled writers, from the most illustrious to the most insipid, are nothing more than domesticated cattle, producing, at best, official poetry, and the same goes more generally for prose, with its slavish, foul-smelling herds of writers, starry-eyed lovers of their own language, culture and history. Now that I'm on the topic, let me add that all travel literature, whether it involves exile or mere tourism, makes me literally puke, and when I think of the sly deceptions we call origins or roots, and of all this pathetic poetry that it inevitably engenders, there is only one notion that comes to my mind: *ball and chain*. People drag their roots around like a ball and chain, you won't find an exiled writer who doesn't drag his roots around like a big old ball and chain that he can't seem to let go of, which is why you'd better let go of yours, especially since our own roots, our origins, and our language are essentially bastardized. Once you've crossed the borders of this fucked up country, this departure will be a golden opportunity for you to unload it all for good, the chance of a lifetime for you to finally acquire the *ontological privilege* of not having any roots or origins or fixed culture. Not belonging to anything or anyone, that just has to be gratifying, Selber. Something to treasure above all else (but Roman didn't have this opportunity, the opportunity to bury his origins for good, to reject his mother tongue and finally renounce everything he *might* be; no, he is still a prisoner, I believe, of this bastardized thing that probably destroyed him in the end). "Here it comes, watch this, it's the last scene, it's the tear-jerker, quick, look." I had every reason to curse this trip, it's all so unreasonable and the idea of spending a few more hours in the company of this unwieldy seat-mate makes me literally nauseous. This guy, whose name I can't remember (he only just introduced himself a moment ago), continues to order drink after drink, there's not a flight attendant who passes without his asking for yet another whiskey or vodka or gin. It's all free, he feels compelled to say, it's all free so why not enjoy it. No sooner had we taken off than he'd already ordered his first drink, and barely an hour into the flight this mustachioed boor was already on his fourth glass. If my calculations are correct, this means he must have already downed about seven or eight in a couple hours, though I can't be sure. This salesman (he made sure I knew that right away, but I'll be starting my own business soon, he hastened to add), this obnoxious salesman has quite simply guzzled a good liter of alcohol all by himself in less than two or three hours, and since he came on board has been utterly content just to drink and eat and sleep. For ten years now, I've spared myself this kind of unpleasantness, ten years since I last travelled, during which I've been striving to put down roots, to resist the siren song of this change of scene that everyone's so crazy about, more than ten years since I stopped thinking about this country I'm about to return to as *a stranger* and that Roman will always embody despite himself. I was right to have decided to never return, even on vacation, I'd resolved (and had succeeded) in definitively blocking this time out of my memory, and again was right to do so. For over ten years I have considered myself cured or recovering, and have never seriously thought about it all again, about Roman, his endless harangues, his mongrel language, his fucked up country, as he said. I'd be wrong if I said it's been easy, I still remember how hard I tried at the beginning; but after a while we forget, we create alternative pasts, it even becomes second nature, then we stop obsessing and we *move on to something else.* We move on to something else, we cease belonging to our past, to what took place, to what is basically dead; we move on to something else and *we try to build a new language from scratch.* We build ourselves an artificial language to escape the indecipherable chaos of the past, and then we try to learn how to think again, something that this mustachioed jerk to my right is preventing me from doing at the moment. We try to control our own lives, but in reality there's no escaping the first slob that grabs hold of you, and this particularly unwieldy specimen is preventing me, without even knowing it of course, from getting a grip on my life. We are constantly disrupted, dismembered and annihilated by the first jerk we happen upon, in fact his mere presence prevents us from getting a grip on our lives, and not once have I managed to completely ignore such nuisances and probably never will. You're in the flow or on a path to something specific, and you believe you're on the right track, and then guys like this one, like this repulsive mustachioed peddler, they come and toss a spanner in the works. *Even our thought process, in other words, what we hold to be positively original, doesn't belong to us at all, in reality it belongs to whoever got there first, and it's precisely this first comer who steers us without our noticing.* Not only does the first comer steer our thought process, not only does he interrupt or derail it, but in reality the first comer literally takes possession of our thoughts to the point of reducing us to mere parrots. Finally, we're no more than puppets and all of humanity the ventriloquist, and none of our thoughts, feelings, nothing that we mistakenly believe as being strictly personal actually belongs to us. Now that I've put this line of reasoning into words, now that I really think about it, I'm even more aware that everything I've just now said isn't mine either, I don't have authorship over it, as they say. These are things that Roman pondered long before me, things he told me about a few years ago now, that I'm merely reproducing here more or less faithfully. But it very often happens that we delude ourselves into believing that our thoughts are original, that we owe nothing to anyone, we often so successfully internalize what others have said that we believe it to be our own, sometimes we even convince ourselves that it's really the others that are mimicking our every thought, but in reality we owe everything to them, from that first comer to the most intimate acquaintance, in reality we are only infinitely hollow containers in which the thoughts, feelings, and behaviors of others come to die, and that's the truth.

"What nationality are you? Alright, in that case you'll need to fill out this form here, they'll be asking you for it at arrival." I've always hated filling out forms, said Roman the day we enrolled at the university together. Ever since I was a little kid, as they say with that revolting, misty-eyed nostalgia, ever since I knew how to write, I've always loathed filling out personal information forms. From the first time forward, I've never enjoyed filling them out, frankly I find them embarrassing (I too have thought of them as being pretty embarrassing). Not only did I not enjoy it, said Roman, not only have I never experienced any sort of pride in performing this task, such attitudes are inconceivable to me, but I saw them as instruments of torture, pure and simple. But in this fucked up country more than any other, we've always loved personal information forms (and we will love them forever, even a hundred years from now), these humiliating bits of paper are what matters most here, and I'm tempted to say that these records constitute the foundations of our so-called civilization. This information is only for reference purposes, they've told us since our childhood, since primary school, but in reality we know perfectly well, at least I myself have always known, that the purpose here is not to reference, as they say, but to obtain the most *exhaustive* information they can. From very early on I understood that filling out these forms was going to be something excruciatingly painful, as far as I remember I have never engaged in this exercise without experiencing a sense of panic. I knew very well that the profile likely to emerge from these supposed for-reference-only bits of paper would be shabby or at least not very reassuring or even normal; I also knew I would start seeming suspicious to them, they'd start eyeing me strangely and finally cast me out for good. As soon as I finished filling out my forms, I knew that they'd look at me differently; in fact as soon as I took up my pen, I knew my world was collapsing forever. Quite frankly, these personal information forms ruined my childhood and my teen years, too, said Roman, every time I had to do it, you could be sure those forms would be thoroughly humiliating, those forms they would underhandedly announce as merely for reference purposes turned out to have devastating long-term consequences. My mother also knew what was going on, knew exactly what caused such unease, my mother knew very well that it was impossible for me to tell the truth on these forms. More accurately, she also had me believe that it was improper to tell the truth. My mother thus explicitly encouraged me to lie, at a time when I was obviously unable to argue. My mother believed that by telling the truth I would arouse suspicion, incriminating looks or signs of pity, Roman said that day, maybe she was right, it hardly matters now, but it's my own mother who instilled in me this sense of shame, with its inevitable deceit. She knew and quite simply delivered the command, since at that age you can't distinguish command from counsel, to brazenly lie while filling out these forms. Tell them he's an international businessman, my mother advised, tell them he's often away on international business, tell them that global business is the reason he's travelling so much, and that his job comes first, this is what my mother taught me to say. Most importantly, don't tell them what he actually does, which, as you'll learn that later, is something to be ashamed of, and if I may, let me tell you, my son, that what he does is in a way amateurish, this is what she saw fit to add. You must learn to keep a secret, my mother always repeated, what happens at home isn't anyone else's business, *the most important thing in the life of a tightly knit family is their ability to keep a secret, because a well-kept secret is the guarantee of a tightly knit family.* What he does or doesn't do has to remain a secret known only to us, it's no one else's business, this is how my mother prepared me for the ordeal of the information forms. Now that these ordeals are behind me, said Roman the day that we enrolled at the university, now that I'm free to fill out these forms all by myself, I think that maybe these forms are purely for reference purposes after all and that it's my mother who made such a big deal out of it. Now that I think about them, these forms were indeed only for reference purposes, and it's actually my mother who was ashamed of what he did or didn't do, it's actually, now that I think of it discerningly in hindsight, my mother who passed on to me the fear of personal information forms. You might say my mother instilled shame and deceit and fear in me, she was the one who set the scene so that I would come to feel such tremendous unease every time I was faced with the most trivial written form. At five or six years of age we don't realize, we are never aware of things that can cause shame, which is why at this age we spontaneously experience the same shame as our parents. Justified or not, we experience the same shame as our parents, the same shame and hatreds, and that's the truth. Our parents, our dear father or mother, handed down their shame to us for life, they've passed on their frustrations and their hatred, none of which came from us, at five or six years of age, you can't reasonably be ashamed of things you aren't even aware of. It's my mother, there can be no doubt, she's the one who told me what I needed to know that day, said Roman, who unloaded on me the full weight of her petty shame, her inferiority complexes and minor frustrations, left to my own devices, I would never have felt the slightest unease at the idea of filling out the altogether innocuous personal information forms, and now I think I can even say that it was my mother who filled out these forms for me, that ultimately it was she who was ashamed of what he was or wasn't doing, that it was she who lied on each line that I filled in, it was my mother, not me, who was overcome by psychosomatic cramps at the idea of having to explain her choices. It goes without saying that parents don't take responsibility for any of their choices, that they hate having to admit to any of their many mistakes, which is why secrecy is the rule, why they literally terrorize their children with their fucking cult of secrecy (I realized myself, a few months after this conversation, how effectively oppressive secrecy felt to the person on the receiving end of confidences, or to be exact, how the secret, beyond the natural pressure it exerts on its victim, embodied this very subtle way of absorbing the other into the hideously expansive bosom of our privacy. This is why, in all cases, I refused to respect anyone's right to secrecy, such that, as soon as anyone asked me to keep a secret, I immediately expelled it from my mind. The craftier among you might say that the more a secret is given away, the more it is shared, broadcast, and even distorted, the more the privacy of its originator gets pumped up and expanded, infinitely multiplied, and by doing so, absorbs those same people who thought they could resist by sowing the secret to the wind. Unrestrained circulation of secrecy is the very definition of transparency. But to be honest, I thought while sipping the last drops of my glass of sparkling water, to be quite honest, every time you hear anything, whether in confidence or picked at random, consider it an assault, a rape, an invasion as underhanded as it is brutal). Don't be a fool, my mother was always telling me, don't you dare *betray* your family by giving away the secrets that we've always guarded with our lives, family is what's most important in life, and if shame ever descends upon this family it will be your own fault. A close-knit family is about keeping its secrets, first and foremost she said to me at the age of five or six, as long as we—and that means you too—are able to keep our secrets, our beautiful family, already so tightly knit, will be tighter still. Now that I'm old enough to think more or less by myself, said Roman, I believe I spent the better part of my childhood tightening our family, which was already supremely, hermetically, hideously tight-knit. If I were to briefly summarize how our family functioned, I would say that we accumulated secrets for a very specific purpose: to remain firmly united and to capitalize on our tremendous cohesion. In other words, secrets, and the systematic deceptions that they imply, were like glue to us, like good thick layers of glue that would make our already close-knit family even closer. And by accumulating well-kept secrets, said Roman, the day that we were lined up at the registration desk, by pathologically stockpiling secrets, you end up not talking about anything with anybody, and then very naturally become aloof and mistrustful, and by the same logic, finally take refuge in absolute silence. "Could you help me fill out this green information form, I'm not used to these things." I remember that day very clearly, it was a Monday morning, and we were lining up to enroll at university, most of all I very clearly remember the gist of what Roman told me about his fear of forms. Time will no doubt disjoint or alter everything Roman said that morning, and I've rendered everything he said in my own language with my own words, but I think I got the gist of what he meant. As I recall it, however lucid he may have been, Roman once again ended up lying on his college enrollment forms. Despite everything he'd just confided—for the first time, I believe—he still hadn't managed to overcome his shame, his lies, his fears, and the personal information forms, even so many years later, still had the same effect on him. These situations were occurring several years later and always resulted in the same effect, which was, if I can trust what I read that morning, that his mother, in a way, was still filling out those forms for him. Despite the years, Roman was still putting down the same information, meaning the same lies covering up the same shameful secrets, and I believe that it was his mother, from beyond the grave, who was still driving him to lie about certain things no matter how trivial. Even dead and gone, his mother was still dictating all the data to provide on his registration form that morning, from beyond the grave she got him to write lies from top to bottom, once again managing to preserve certain secrets that Roman ought to have purged himself of by then. With my own eyes, I saw that Roman had written, *as bright as day* international businessman; from a few feet away, I could see the total lack of expression on his face as he filled out his form. I remember that morning so vividly, when Roman didn't even try to hide the fact that it was his dead mother filling out the registration form for him, he didn't even bother to conceal how tight her grip on him was, even from the grave. I remember that even beyond the restraint normally exercised in such circumstances, Roman suppressed an intense sense of relief the day he buried his mother. At the time he believed that everything would change, he naïvely believed he was finally out from under the spell of the closely guarded family secrets that had accumulated throughout his life once he was rid of his mother, rid of her shame, rid of her frustrations and her lies that were hers alone. I feel free at last, he said a few days after his mother's funeral; you'd think her death would leave me totally indifferent given the circumstances, but on the contrary, her death has plunged me into a sort of rapture, something akin to *tantric serenity.* "Is this German or Dutch here in parentheses?" People weep profusely at their parents' death; fortunately, it also happens that sometimes people abstain from shedding the few requisite tears while burying their parents, but I honestly think that the day I buried my mother was undisputedly one of the happiest days of my life. I think that in dying my mother accomplished a very special act, it was even, to be quite honest, the most noble act she had ever accomplished in her entire life. Ever since he'd left on a business trip, my mother had everything so organized down to the tiniest detail that I would literally suffocate under the corpulence of the cult of the close-knit family, the cult of the family always united against the enemy from without, the cult of the reclusive family bound by the shackles of motherly love. In fact, even before he left on his business trip, my mother had already very knowingly paved the way, my imprisonment had already started long before that tragic event, Roman confided, a couple days after the funeral. Scarcely had I emerged from the sordid placental prison than my mother began plotting and weaseling and scheming for him to leave on a one-way business trip, said Roman on the day of the wake; no sooner did *my* tiny skull appear soaking in *her* excrement and *her* blood than my father's fate was sealed. In other words, ever since my birth, if not before, I was already locked in conflict with my mother, and would be for a long time to come. Rummaging through her belongings once, I discovered what she had been plotting all along; to be even more exact, it was when I read my birth announcement written in her own hand that I finally realized that none of this had happened by chance, that everything had been scrupulously planned since the beginning. Skimming the bottom of the handwritten announcement, I saw my mother's first name in *capital letters* and my father's first name in *parentheses*, and it was then I realized that this long *one-on-one* with my mother had begun long ago, had been ardently desired and systematically coveted. My father's fate was sealed the day his first name was placed in parentheses, as was mine, sealed and delivered, because I was already set to become, for many years, the hostage of an *overreaching* motherly love (as it turns out, what happened that day we enrolled in the university together confirmed that he was still hostage to this motherly love). "This is so stupid, it asks us here whether we brought any weapons on board! I'd love to meet the genius who designed this form." A woman as shrewd as my mother would have wanted my father to be an international businessman, or an internationally renowned doctor, or even an international bureaucrat, for that matter; a woman as shrewd as my mother wanted above all a husband with a respectable profession, a lucrative profession, a profession fitting the standards of the country, in short, a simply *splendid* profession, said Roman. Shrewd as she was, my mother knew from the outset that her marriage would end in bitter, resounding failure, and in all honesty she could not reasonably have been unaware that the man she was preparing to spend a lifetime with, as they still said back then, simply had no job skills to speak of, could not possibly measure up to her hopes and schemes, didn't fit the bill, as they say. A man who did what he did couldn't fulfill her hopes and schemes, Roman told me the day of the wake; there is simply no way that a man whose profession is contemptible by definition can play the role of husband for keeps, which is why I so readily say that my father's fate was sealed from the get-go, just as mine was settled from the start, meaning long before his first name was placed in parentheses and, thus, long before my birth. Now that things have gradually come into focus, I can see that it was long before my mother was married that my one-on-one with her had already been plotted out, and I would even venture to say that she had been planning this one-on-one since her puberty, and it would have happened whether my father had been involved or not. It mattered very little who it was, said Roman on that same day of the wake, such considerations are utterly fruitless and at no point interfered with the little schemes of a woman as shrewd as my mother, and such considerations in any case can hardly explain why I became, for those very long and painful years, may I repeat, the hostage of a *blindly* overreaching motherly love. Whoever the progenitor was, this one-on-one would have taken place no matter what, and now that I'm entitled to speak freely, as it were, continued Roman, now that my mother is moldering away six feet under, I'm thinking that the term one-on-one itself is but a pale reflection of our relationship. I think the term one-on-one, which usually describes extremely stressful or painful situations, or what they rather timidly call *traumatic* in the psychologist's vocabulary, proves to be, in my exemplary case, extremely reductive, I seriously think we would be committing a great injustice toward my late mother to say that the only thing she could muster up was a pathetic, workaday one-on-one. Not only would it be an irreparable injustice to even talk about it, as she's no longer here to defend herself, but it would also shamefully undermine her prodigious ability to unleash the ruthless frenzy of her overreaching love, Roman specified without the slightest irony. Even if only to preserve her memory and the memory of her grand accomplishments, I am compelled to use a more telling term, a more suitable term, at least a term that's less reductive, and I see, now that I have to find the right word on the fly, I can't find a better expression just now than *huis clos* (I remember clearly that at the time he used that term, Roman had just discovered the theater of Jean-Paul Sartre). Once he left on his business trip, meaning since my mother finally had her hands free, as they say, I was then entitled not to an inoffensive one-on-one but to a *huis clos*, just the two of us, behind closed doors, no exit, said Roman that day. She brought me into this world, she chased out the intruder, and then immediately shoved me into an inescapable Machiavellian trap. This woman simply pushed me into a trap at birth, and from start to finish, exactly from the day she was born until her recent death, she diabolically devised this perfectly infernal trap, this perfectly infernal trap that over time led to several years of one-on-ones, more precisely to several years of airtight, no-exit *huis clos*. Since my birth, my life has been lived in the service of *a perfectly hermetic huis clos,* continued Roman, of a *huis clos* that was constantly force-fed these vital family secrets we all so obscenely worshipped. Obviously, any information, any rumor or hearsay that our close-knit family picked up, from the most trivial to the most consequential, needed first to assume the aspect of *revelation,* then logically be stamped with the seal of secrecy. Whatever the nature of this information my late mother managed to pick up, imagine or transmit, regardless of the tone in which this information was disclosed, my mother always took care to explain that what she was about to tell us was nothing short of an immense revelation whose mysterious contents should naturally be kept secret. So now that I think about it, this logorrheic secretion of shameful secrets was probably not triggered by the intruder's timely departure on some business trip, no, the abominable intruder who had shamefully deserted us like the coward he was, according to my mother, was but one of the many breeding grounds of these delirious secrets—which we all had to keep alive no matter what. At the age of five or six, trust isn't the issue, said Roman suddenly that day of the wake, at five or six, or even ten, you can't possibly be aware that keeping a secret, regardless of its relevance or justification or basis in fact, that keeping a secret is a matter of trust, because in reality, at that age, keeping a secret or not is above all a matter of love, of proving how much you love, or more plainly put, it's about fear of abandonment. If you repeat it, I will never tell you anything ever again, said my late mother, repeating would mean that you don't love your mother who literally *sacrifices* everything for you, repeating would simply mean that your mother wouldn't love you anymore, this is how my mother blackmailed me into providing endless proof of my love, here is especially how my mother, whose Machiavellian torture techniques so easily pass for selflessness to anyone who knows only her public face, locking me into a *huis clos* that I was *afraid* to escape from anyway. Of course, Roman said that day, of course, the way my mother construed things, everything she did was all about *sacrifice*, and there is no action, however trivial or basic, that wasn't immediately and conspicuously claimed by her as a unique and absolute sacrifice, in other words, a sacrifice that no mother, however loving, would be prepared to make. You might say that my mother was hands down the undefeated *world champion* of sacrifice, and that other contenders could only wish they even came close to the self-sacrificing record she has set. For a woman as loving as my mother, there was no way that so many daily sacrifices could be accomplished in the dignity of silence, continued Roman, nor could so many sacrifices, for a woman as Machiavellian as my mother, go eternally unrewarded; they were indeed the result of such bravery, such magnanimity and devotion in sacrifice—daily, she reiterated—that they absolutely deserved their just reward, which is why all of these innumerable so-called sacrifices that she droned on about day in day out demanded, according to my mother, always demanded more respect and more love, which is to say more *gratitude* and more *deference.* My mother designed the perfect trap and then she shoved me in at an early age, she knew from the start that this airtight *huis clos* that she had locked me into had to rest upon some solid fundaments, on some cunningly crafty fundaments, of which the now hackneyed term of emotional blackmail is, in the end, an imperfect but significant illustration. Actually, the whole point of this emotional blackmail, whose cults of secrecy and gratitude are the very *lifeblood,* stated Roman insistently, the whole point of this emotional blackmail resides in its tremendous ability to generate voluntary servitude. My mother's whole educational agenda consisted in formatting my brain for emotional blackmail even before the actual words were spoken, said Roman that day. Then, once past the early years during which this constant intimidation was very openly stated, once past these fruitful years of training during which she so tirelessly sacrificed, my mother no longer felt any more need to actually inflict emotional blackmail: the process collapsed, faded, then disappeared altogether, leaving behind only the grandeur of the punishment itself. Beyond a certain point, my mother could legitimately benefit from these years of training that she provided without the slightest complaint, once this painstaking but indispensable time was over, my mother could at last enjoy the fruits of her labor, the behavior pattern she ingrained into the son she so insanely adored. And this pattern, Roman soon added, naturally this pattern involved anticipating emotional blackmail, in other words, the pattern of permanent resignation, the pattern of voluntary servitude. Twenty years of voluntary servitude, repeated Roman several times that supposedly tragic day of the wake, this diabolically asphyxiating *huis clos* that my mother sentenced me to steadily consolidated over several years, and nothing could loosen the grip of my voluntary servitude. But now that the precise term has finally welled up from who knows what depths, I believe that it would be intellectually dubious to characterize the thing as a steadily consolidating *huis clos*, resumed Roman; to characterize it as a *huis clos*—however diabolically asphyxiating—would amount not only to misjudging or underestimating or insulting my mother, who (I will never tire of repeating) was a shrewd woman capable of the most extraordinary feats, but it would most especially give a very unflattering picture, or at least one that falls far short of describing these twenty beautiful years of absolute abomination. In his anger that evening, or was it perhaps his euphoria, Roman used a term to describe those years, the term *incarceration*, or more precisely, a deadly, totalitarian, incarceration. This abomination of a woman locked me up for several years, he confided on the day of the wake, and almost never, to be quite honest, not even once did I manage to get free from her pincer-like grasp. Scarcely had I been expelled from the womb, no sooner had I tumbled into what would prove to be her own hermetically sealed world, than my mother suddenly and brutally had me in a stranglehold. I realize only now that during all those painful years, that is to say my entire childhood and adolescence, and a sizable chunk of my adult life, I was caught in this brutal stranglehold. After all those years of unspeakable torture, after all those years of voluntary servitude whose seriousness I was yet to truly understand, I now realize more clearly that, from the beginning, I was absolutely trapped in that stranglehold that my mother took pleasure in perfecting, of course, in adjusting it to suit the circumstance. I think that I can now say, as she is no longer here to deny it, that my mother clearly didn't want a son or a daughter or anything of the sort—a cat or a canary, for example—such a second-rate desire doesn't suit a woman as refined, as sophisticated, as shrewd as my mother. What she yearned for, said Roman, what she had yearned for from the very start, had to take the form of an *object*, any object would do, but preferably malleable, easy to get into a stranglehold. Banking on human beings, in other words, on very unreliable material, was not on my mother's agenda during these long, painful years of voluntary servitude, which is why I believe that, during those long and painful years of voluntary servitude, I was nothing but an object in her fierce vice-grip that she alone controlled. It was only several weeks after hearing this monologue that I myself came to realize how much the act of resisting this onslaught of motherly love, especially when these repeated aggressions are lurking somewhere beneath the veneer of self-sacrifice, how much this resistance was a matter of physical survival. What had been initially triggered by pure empathy toward Roman eventually acquired a certain autonomy and my own parents, who probably didn't operate at the same unspeakable level as Roman's mother, naturally became my worst enemies. That my own parents never met the same standards of depravity that Roman's mother prided herself in wasn't the point, ultimately, and the question as to whether or not they had ever tried to crush me couldn't abort or deflect the agenda that I'd set for myself: to disown my family. A person should never be burdened by his family, and everything that the very notion of family conjures up has mainly to do with shame, however well-behaved or educated or open a particular family might seem. We'll never get anywhere, as they say, as long as even a spark of filial emotion is driving us, nor can we foresee ever becoming anything of substance as long as the residue of this filial emotion hasn't been completely dislodged from our memories; this is what I was thinking to myself as I waited for one of the airplane's toilets to free up. Dislodging memory isn't enough, we must denounce everything that's primitive and bestial about families, not only must we respond to the slightest filial urge with hatred, but we must fight such urges to the death with everything in our power. Fight parents to the death, I said to myself as I cooled my heels in front of the door to the toilet. Fight them to the death and never, no matter how extreme their distress, never hesitate to bring out their bitterness. Psychoanalysis wants this fight against our own filial emotions to be motivated by all this Oedipus business or a case of an unresolved castration complex, I thought as I finally got my turn in the loo, it's even one of the more popular psychoanalytic teachings, in other words, one of the more formidable clichés deployed by the family to defuse the death struggle anyone might attempt to wage against it. Instead of muzzling it, psychoanalysis has deeply reinforced the family's lethal power, it has, now that I think about it, absolutely preempted the salubrious struggle that everyone should be waging against his own family, come what may. By propagating its noxious Oedipal theory, psychoanalysis has reduced to the level of unimpeachable cliché the motives for what ought to be a fight to the finish against the family, and *especially* against mothers, if not *exclusively* against mothers, and in doing so, despite its earlier nebulous intentions, has brutally destroyed the individual in favor of the family—that family, ever since it surrendered to the tyranny of mothers, has shown no signs of imminent collapse, as the idiots had all once predicted it would. Moreover, today this psychoanalytic cliché itself has given way to an even sillier commonplace, a somehow more literary kind of cliché, to a cliché that inevitably makes a laughing stock out of anyone who speaks out against the institution of the family. Today, whoever dares to describe in more or less shrill tones the torment inflicted by a family unit, of any family unit, if you look close enough, anyone who tries his hand at demolishing everything utterly lethal that the family represents, will be labeled with the same supreme epithet: ridiculous. And yet in reality, as long as the language of the father, and more especially the language of the mother, finds an extension in our own language, as long as their lethal language continues to resonate into a future when our parents are long gone, the paths to individuation will remain indefinitely blocked, this is what I was thinking as I returned to my seat that had been encroached upon once again by my bulbous neighbor. In his moments of miraculous lucidity, long after his mother's funeral, Roman used to say that he quite obviously had not yet managed to slip out of the maternal stranglehold. He repeated that he had never, not even for an instant, managed to escape the bonds of servitude that his mother had imposed on him so early. Obviously, my mother had everything to gain from a situation like this, Roman said shortly before my departure, and I am tempted to believe, he said, that my mother, true to her usual Machiavellian contortions, had willfully locked us into a country among people at war. Although my mother had the opportunity to seek a safe haven for us, as they say, although she clearly had the means to take us somewhere abroad, Roman clarified, my mother still preferred to keep us there, which is to say, in a country full of people on a killing spree. That we were constantly forced to flee, that the war forced us to move into areas of the city temporarily spared from murder, that we had been virtually incapable of putting down roots or establishing ourselves anywhere, must certainly have suited my mother to perfection. Putting down roots somewhere was the one certain nightmare that haunted my mother's sleepless hours, which is why she was always ready to lug us all from one side of the country to the other, and why, I'm now sure, that my mother always chose, as a supposed safe haven, the regions, districts, and neighborhoods where everyone predicted the next scene of destruction would take place. Roman was convinced that the incessant relocations he had been subjected to were what sustained and perpetuated the *huis clos* that his mother had locked him into so early. Nothing is more conducive to a *huis clos* than a country at war, he said; absolutely nothing can ensure the survival of a *huis clos* as well as a highly mobile, chaotic and openly hostile environment, in other words an environment in which only a pathologically loving mother could protect us. The war magnified the enemy from without—against which our close-knit family defended itself tooth and nail—to the point of rendering it astonishingly abstract, he added; in a country at war, danger was so frighteningly widespread that everyone, from the next door neighbor to the closest relative, was designated by my mother as the outside enemy. On the pretense of shielding us against the outside enemy, which is to say almost everyone, my mother would greatly fortify the foundations of the *huis clos* she'd trapped me in so early, and obviously nothing, especially not a war of the most terrorizing and despicable kind, nothing could have been better for extending indefinitely our honeymoon of shared confinement. Under these very skillfully prepared and carefully maintained conditions, concluded Roman that day, under these conditions, there was ultimately nothing I could do but put down roots *in* my mother. While squirming in my narrow economy-class seat, still struggling to keep my right leg from falling asleep, I noticed that almost all the passengers aboard the plane were slumbering away at present, that each one's sleeping habits were on view for all to see, that we had at last reached that special degree of intimacy that allows people to openly display their body's slightest twitch—the kind of exhibitionism granted only after a long prelude of reticence, modesty or correctness. In short, I thought, while turning the overhead light back on, they basically would have me believe that we've known each other for a while at this point, that we've all gotten pretty close by now, and therefore, what was mine, my seat, my field of vision, my peace and quiet, was finally theirs. "Did I snore?" Roman often recalled those sleepless nights where, instead of going to bed like everyone else, he had to stay up and whistle, constantly varying his tunes, to interrupt, though never for very long, his mother's thunderous snores. Not only did I have to deal with the crashing of bombs that would rain down on our underground shelter for hours at a stretch, said Roman, not only did I jump in teeth-chattering fear and plug my ears every time that this incredibly loud noise pounded my eardrums, but I was then subjected to a far more irritating sort of noise pollution, much closer at hand, located, in fact, just a few inches from my ear canal: the peculiarly *percussive* snoring of my mother. We slept—well, she slept mostly—side by side, curled up against each other in the rotting interior of our car, continued Roman, we slept stifled by the sticky heat, in the company of a colony of starving mosquitoes, we slept blanketed in thick layers of gray dust, we slept breathing in the unpleasant odors of sweat, gasoline, and flatulence; but we slept mostly *in* the snoring of my mother. And this remarkable snoring, these remarkable *nasal detonations* that would assault my ears and gradually crescendo, peaking in periods of stage four sleep, as *the experts* call it, increasing in quality, purity, rhythm, and there were even times, quite often in fact, said Roman, correcting himself, that the intensity of these detonations would mingle with the sharp, metallic bursts of precision bombs, almost entirely eclipsing this already preternatural din. Night after night I managed to eke out a few hours of very poor sleep, two or three at most, wrested from this polyphonic storm that bore down like a clamp on my head. Every night, insisted Roman, every night I trembled with fear *and* fatigue, a very special fatigue that only insomniacs know, every night I accomplished the feat of having nightmares without ever or only rarely, closing my eyes. This constant and impartially distributed nervous pressure, was such, continued Roman, that I was losing control of my movements and I even surprised myself, several times, applying little kicks and even slaps to this horror show of a woman snoring away at my side—alas, without success. It was only after three weeks of hallucinogenic insomnia, during which, among other dubious honors, I earned the vague reputation of the naughty little son who beat up his poor victim of a mother—a moral status from which she derived, incidentally, much of what she liked to call "her rights," —it was only after three or four weeks, repeated Roman, that the neighbors, obviously troubled at the sight of my ghostly and hostile face all day long, offered to let me sleep in their spacious van. Lucky for me, my neighbors were so insistent that, for the first time, my mother had no choice, rejoiced Roman: she would have obviously preferred to keep me stuffed into her perky blue car a little longer, she would have had no qualms about holing up for another few months in what she'd probably come to think of as a *bridal suite*, she of all people, who saw those bombings as no more than an excuse to extend our stay in this hellish war-torn country, she finally had to relent, going against all of her systems of thought, she finally gave in and let herself be separated, temporarily mind you, from her son. "Did you know that chameleons could get to be that big?" Naturally, said Roman, naturally the blessed respite, as they say, lasted only a short time, and my mother, who was clearly having trouble tolerating this relative distancing, this heartbreak, as she probably called it, began to prowl around the van at night, instead of offering, if not to the world then at least to our various neighbors, what she could do with such exceptional talent: snore. Like no other. Instead of sleeping like a freight train, as she had done uninterruptedly for the last three or so weeks, instead of saturating the interior of the car with those deafening detonations that she alone knew how to produce, she simply took to prowling, said Roman, she began prowling and scraping at the windows of the van. She prowled around and scratched and stuck her nose up against the window every night, and for a whole week she prowled, then scratched, then stuck her nose against the glass. "No way would you be able to see those chameleons in their natural element!" Sick. To put an end to this separation that was driving my now hysterical mother to utter distraction, that horrible little fireplug of a woman (according to my recollections, which are unreliable after so many years, she was only about yea tall), who wasn't one to be thwarted for very long, had finally come up with the ultimate trick, the unstoppable ploy, the ruse no one was expecting: getting sick. Getting really, really sick then leveraging the sickness to the *max*, so to speak to extort maximum attention, or maximum compassion, or simply maximum pity, this is how my mother succeeded, once again, said Roman, with a sort of noticeable dejection, in depriving me of a modicum of autonomy, this especially is how she managed to keep me, very firmly and for a good while yet, in her stranglehold. I remember that this *taste*, because it's undeniably a taste, said Roman, that this taste for sickness that had been so finely cultivated over the years by his mother Johanna was yielding diminishing returns, as they say. In early adolescence, at least according to the version he told me when we used to hang out, Roman had allowed himself a few minor acts of incremental rebellion, like for example, going to the movies without his mother, or going to soccer games without his mother, or more unusual still, going to parties without his mother. Of course my mother could neither understand nor tolerate such liberties, which, more generally speaking, were beyond the reach of her reason, whatever reason she may still have possessed at that point, Roman hastened to add, such liberties were simply inconceivable; and once again, it was only thanks to the timely advice, if not the coercive urging on the part of whoever her lover happened to be at the time, that she finally consented, against her better albeit warped judgment, to allow me a few hours, a few very short hours of parole. Sick. It was exactly at this point, when she saw her hysterically beloved son take a few tiny liberties at an altogether appropriate age, it was at this moment that she further refined, almost like a professional, her taste for sickness. That evening (it was shortly before the Christmas holidays if I remember correctly), Roman told me that before fully satisfying her *lust for bed rest*, his mother Johanna had—once again—gotten rid of the intruder who was making sly attempts to separate her, by his mere presence, from her unwholesomely adored son. He told me that evening (we were having drinks at some dive), that the reason why her lover had cleared off, at least that was the official version, meaning the one his mother defended against all evidence to the contrary, that this reason was related to the moral, emotional, and physical well-being of her son. So I've decided, she said, despite all the pain and loneliness and depression that this unfair outcome implies, if I've decided, she said, to show Alfred the door after these few months of complete happiness spent in his company, it's for *your* own good. It's for your own good that Alfred, who always behaved like a perfect *gentleman* with your poor mother, was asked to hit the road, it's only so that you're not disturbed by his presence that the poor man at an undoubtedly great emotional cost, left our home for good. Unlike the little bastard that left us in the lurch, the sneak, Alfred was a wonderful man, a dentist, a man who fully deserved all of the love and sensuality I was capable of offering him. Roman often told me, actually, that his mother always thought of herself as beautiful and attractive and young, she always presumed that everyone else thought so too, that no man could reasonably resist her charm and that she had, after all, *the same needs as every woman.* He told me that these female needs that she dared not mention, out of a sort of false, subtly eloquent modesty, were never called by their exact term, i.e., getting laid; he told me that these female needs were being more and more openly evoked, whether implied or claimed outright as a basic grievance, and that they were increasingly listed in the voluminous catalog of her lamentations. Of course the last thing my mother really wanted was to satisfy these much touted female needs; it was never really about all that, and I am sure of it now, that the only thing that my mother truly lusted after, whenever she raged on about her female needs, that all that she really wanted was further acknowledgement of her status as eternal martyr. I remember that shortly after Johanna's funeral, Roman told me that in terms of sexuality, his mother was content just to scream her frustration without ever attempting to treat it, that is, without ever taking advantage of this supposedly devastating charm she claimed to embody; he told me that in terms of female needs, his mother had found her happiness, as they say, on the television screen. Rather than getting laid and calming her female urges, instead of leveraging her seduction capital with men, she covertly watched erotic films on television with the lights off. Every Saturday and Sunday my mother went through hours of erotic films on television, said Roman, my mother consumed them with greed and in absolute secrecy, *she thought*, she would watch the most vulgar, mediocre, and unappealing erotic productions on television. If I put an end to all this, she said, to this wonderful love story with a man—a dentist, she insisted—so simply wonderful, if I once again put my own happiness and my own female needs *on hold*, well, know that I did that only for you, for your own stability—for your own good. Naturally none of this was true, said Roman, neither the so-called romance, nor the so-called bliss, nor the so-called perfection that her Alfred embodied—dentist though he may have been. And of course the one reason Alfred hit the road, as my mother said, the one reason that my mother literally forced him to make himself scarce came down to this: Alfred was in the way. Alfred came between us. Alfred might take my place. Alfred might take her place. Alfred might behave like a father. It was unacceptable. "That hostess has a really nice ass!" We tend to believe that history repeats itself in the same terms, it is always an eternal renewal of the same, as the superficial readers of Nietzsche say, that it's this kind of largely predictable permanence that we can always count on. So that's the purpose of history, to not reproduce the same mistakes, to not commit the same blunders, to not keep misbehaving; we need only learn our lessons, we're told, learn our lessons well enough to prevent the worst from happening again. Of course, said Roman, of course history does repeat itself right there in front us, it repeats and taunts us on a daily basis, and we're helpless to control the least event, helpless to avoid history's stutter, as they say, without which history would not be repetition. History repeats itself, Roman maintained, it repeats and taunts us, but never in the same way twice, and that's the truth. The fact that my mother used exactly the same strategies as always, hell-bent on evicting from her life, from my life, anything resembling a father figure, as they say in psychoanalysis, any interference, any *troublemaker*, was perfectly consistent with her contortions, deviousness, and scheming that she had always so liberally apportioned. None of this was new, developing steadily over the years, but as it went it took detours and side roads that were always different. The hidden charm of odium. As Roman's relative freedom was becoming in a manner of speaking legitimate (he would have been around fifteen or sixteen then), Johanna was growing increasingly intolerant of those few moments of respite when they were apart, those off duty hours that the beloved son gradually, almost unnoticeably began appropriating. If I'm to believe Roman's retelling of it back when we were pretty close friends, Johanna's first major home enema dated back to their first serious confrontation: he had missed his curfew by three hours. "I'm crazy about wildlife documentaries, and this one is super." The enema was only the beginning, said Roman, it was only what triggered a regimen of obsessive and ambitious bed rest—the stuff of which the sickest of the legendarily sick is made, as they say. My mother understood very well that to appease her son's unwarranted desire for autonomy, that ingrate, as she liked to call him, in other words to refresh the nevertheless inexhaustible range of her diabolical tricks and her emotional blackmail techniques, she understood, said Roman, that she would have to face the joys of it, for illness, after all, was a joy. I still remember her first cancer, which she survived of course, it was around the time when I first started to get interested in girls my age, Roman told me with nostalgia, it was in the uterus and it was huge, as huge as the frenetic desire that brought it about. My mother took eagerly to her sickbed, in hospitals and especially at home—at first it was mostly at home, that is, in the most visible and cumbersome way possible—she was bedridden until I was nineteen, twenty years old, and not one year, not a single month passed by without her discovering, giddy with delight, a new disease, each more serious and challenging than the last. Thus, she managed in rapid succession, and brilliantly I might add, to not only develop several large and unusual cancers in various parts of her body, including breasts and lymph nodes, but managed just as brilliantly to develop some no less serious collateral pathologies, such as ulcers and other intestinal disorders, osteoporosis, hormonal imbalances or even vile skin diseases. During all these years in bed—during which her techniques of emotional blackmail reached dizzying peaks of perfection and professionalism—during all those years of endless treatments that had probably filled the coffers of several hospitals in the city, during all of these years, as I was saying, my mother felt tended to, pampered and coddled beyond her wildest dreams. While undergoing her first no-frills house-call enema, the urgent need for which had appeared, coincidentally, a few days after that first confrontation, my mother was quick to analyze and understand everything she stood to gain from sickness, and all the attendant tender loving care: the prerogative of great pain—in other words, a *throne.* There is, actually, I thought while fastening my seatbelt, there is nothing more abject than people who suffer or who yearn to suffer. I always thought, and Roman's experience is there to attest, that people who suffer and who are determined to let the world know, do not deserve our sympathy, unless they actually succumb to their atrocious suffering, they deserve no more than our total disregard. There is absolutely no one more ludicrous, more temperamental, and more tyrannical than a person who suffers and enjoys it and who literally *expounds on* it, which is why I am always scrupulously determined to despise all those who suffer a bit too conspicuously. But there is also nothing more repugnant, more appalling than people who suffer in silence, with discretion and dignity, as they say, because these unassuming people reap the admiration of all, keeping silent about their suffering only to better vaunt their dignity. In the end, and perhaps this explains my boundless antipathy for those who suffer greatly, in the end, pain—which itself connotes no *positive value*, no beauty, nor any particular aesthetic—is despicable in every way to the extent it necessarily and unarguably bestows a kind of moral privilege, or moral ascendancy, or moral whatnot, upon anyone who has suffered its so-called slings and arrows. Avoid sufferers like the plague, was my advice to myself, and absolutely deny them any mark of compassion or sympathy or esteem. "It's time for my meds. I confess that I have a little digestion issue that's been messing with my stomach for a while now." Never did my mother feel as pampered, as spoiled, as *princess-like* as when she was in the hospital, said Roman, never, even in her most wanton, wildest dreams had she dared to imagine such devotion, such concern, or such attention—disinterested, she probably thought—for her and her alone. My mother loved, adored, worshipped the hospital because she felt so very good there, because it felt so very much like home to her because she could complain so very much there (it's the very place for it), and no other place in the world—hotel, resort, or bed-and-breakfast, for example, would henceforward find favor in her eyes. My mother, continued Roman with obvious glee, my mother stalked sickness, as a hunter does his prey, she stalked it *religiously*, lovingly, so much that she lived only in expectation, or better, in the hope of the next disease that she might unearth by sheer force of will. There is seemingly no end to the charms of sickness, and the one that my mother was the wildest about, the one she most serially *abused*, but without ever losing her taste for it, one that she wouldn't have been able to do without, in the end—and there's a reason for that—was called drugs. My mother gobbled down her meds the way others might eat chocolate or potato chips, said Roman, she gazed at them lovingly for a few seconds, then sucked on them with the slight shrug of the shoulder, then greedily gulped them down one after the other, or all in one go, never pausing; all the energy that she so *theatrically* deployed to come up with increasingly complicated and hideous diseases found its material reward, its just and immediate reward in this bulimic drug-taking: my mother possessed a certain canine instinct: the effort spent in fetching the stick was immediately rewarded with a treat. Needless to say, her son's altogether timid rebellion by now had assumed the proportions of a genuine illness that the medical profession as a whole also had to address, and for which they had to *militarily* mobilize. Every whim that my mother couldn't satisfy at home, all requests for unconditional devotion that she could not fulfill at home, all of the failures that her ungrateful son was so guilty of at home, everything, absolutely everything, even those much-discussed female needs that she insisted were getting increasingly acute, she transferred all that to the hospital in a wink. Which only created new frustrations that my mother, whose idea of ecstasy involved endless lamentation, was clearly enjoying more and more openly; she managed to find, in no matter what circumstance, and despite the doctor's financial devotion—code for sincerity—she still managed to complain about incompetent physicians, negligent nurses, and of course, her ungrateful son. Unearthing diseases by sheer force of will, theatrically bemoaning her plight and forever blaming everyone around her for it, here in a few words, said Roman, was the method that my late mother used to asphyxiate her son, the medical profession, and the whole world. Now that I'm able to delve more deeply into what Roman had to say about the desires of his bed-stricken mother (my neighbor has finally settled down), I wonder if my own beliefs, my own thoughts, my own opinions about disease, about the almost sacred image and the *favors* that it confers upon its victims, if my own views are truly unique, authentic, and indisputably mine. I am almost certain that the reason this whole issue of sickness popped into my mind and set me thinking can be traced back to Roman and my somewhat altered memory of Roman's *stream of consciousness rants*. For several hours now (I haven't kept count, actually), Roman's words, phrases, and voice have taken over, for several hours now his entire being has spread through every region of my body, and I must confess that I can't distinguish much of anything at this point. I have a very clear sensation, a physical one, in any case, that Roman's brain, mind, and thoughts have gradually replaced my own brain, my mind, and my thoughts, the sensation, again physical, of being nothing more than a transparent *shell of a body* open to the whims and the appetites of others, especially to Roman's. Which of the two of us thinks that disease hasn't lost any of its prestige, more specifically, which of the two of us thinks that the term 'crazy' has never been such a thinly veiled and multi-purpose compliment, which of the two of us thinks that madness, modernity's quirky new aesthetic, which one of us thinks that madness has probably never been as systematically courted and cultivated and flaunted as today, I can't say with any accuracy. Which, Roman or me, which of these two *individuals* is the author of these terse, compelling, and at least in part, pertinent remarks on madness, which of these two individuals is thinking or speaking or soliloquizing at this precise moment, I still couldn't say. Perhaps we are talking at the same time, *one inside the other.* In reality I can't tell the difference anymore. And yet, I'd promised myself that never again, as long as I live, would I ever again for any reason yield to nostalgia, or to any kind of moronic contemplation of the past, or to the teary-eyed, maudlin rekindling of this or that person's memory. Especially since Roman will always embody—in spite of himself, that is, ten years down the road—my abysmal cesspool of a homeland. I had promised to never think of it ever again, to stop feeling sorry for it even in secret, to never speak their language. It's this trip. This fucking trip that I should have known better to cancel. I don't know which end is up, and I sure can't figure out what ever made me think that any of these thoughts were mine—or conversely, Roman's. I wonder if it is even possible to identify where our thoughts actually come from, our inspirations of the moment or our intuitions, I thought while unbuckling my seatbelt, I wonder if the frenzied urge to detect any source for the least of our thoughts, the most fleeting of our momentary inspirations, the least of our intuitions is not utterly foolish. Wanting at all costs to claim authorship of this or that thought, wanting to identify with certainty the exact source of this other thought or that one, all of course in the vain hope of discovering our own creative power, this must surely border on the densest of stupidities, this is what also characterizes the kind of nauseating pretension that the middle classes are positively dripping with. Now that I think of it, I'm almost certain that the ideas of origin, of descent or heritage, which do very clearly underlie the way we perceive and worship individuality, that these ideas are quite simply deadly. We must be positively crazy for contriving to not only unearth the origin of the least of our thoughts, but also, more broadly, to believe that originality or even singularity, otherwise known as fatally decorative concepts, are what make up the individual. No one is unique, no one is original; no one can reasonably and in any manner whatsoever lay claim to individuality. So why strive for it? Why strive to keep alive the illusion of a so-called singularity that clearly doesn't exist, which probably never existed, or never existed beyond the confines of the infinitely pathetic and petty middle class mind. Be yourself, we are learnedly advised, very learnedly even, be yourself or discover who you are or become what you are, here is the great triple lie that we've been fed for years on end. For years on end we've been very explicitly summoned to become what we are, for years and even centuries, philosophers, educators and writers have been gently intimating that we must strive to be nothing other than ourselves—and no one else, need I specify. Be yourself and everything will be fine, they tell us; become what you are and you'll be at peace, discover who you are and you'll never hunger for more. All of these people, all of these celebrated thinkers, philosophers, and artists, have filled our heads for centuries with their fatally flawed concepts of identity, individuality, and uniqueness, all these people, who still enjoy today the inflated prestige that's been in reality extorted from countless generations of ignoramuses, yes all these people have laid us low, crushed us and scattered our remains, even from beyond their graves. We can expect little from these supposedly disinterested calls for a higher wisdom, there is strictly nothing to gain from ideas as false and fatal as that of our own individuality, our own identity, our own uniqueness. This is because, I thought as I snuck a glance at my traveling companion, who still seemed enthralled by the wildlife documentary on his monitor (his dazed expression verging on stupor), for what's really at issue here isn't the terms individuality, identity or uniqueness—these criminally widespread terms don't correspond to any reality—but the particular adjective that's most often attached to them, or, when not expressly mentioned, serves as their exclusive theoretical substratum. There is no such thing as one's own. No 'own' we can own, in any case, and that's the truth. So then there's nothing to be gained from these ideas, and the ground where they bud and flower is nothing but a steaming pile of manure. Keep as far away from yourself as you can, as far as you can from the representations we have of ourselves, far, far away from everything that feeds the obnoxious fantasies of the individual, from notions of self-esteem or your own individuality, that's what I swore to do. And you'll be better off, a whole lot better off, by working hard at not being yourself, by being just about anything else, *say, a table, a dog, someone else, rather than yourself.* "I'd love another little gin, actually, thanks." I can't believe that this annoying lump in the next seat is still managing to order and knock back a single drop more of alcohol, gratis or otherwise. I seem to be the only one who has noticed that this guy is probably on his tenth or eleventh glass of gin or vodka or wine—I've lost count. Judging from the dazed bovine look in his eyes, and the sense of release with which he greeted his umpteenth drink of the day, I'm thinking that he must be absolutely determined to raise his blood alcohol count to record-breaking levels, or maybe even trying to replace his last drop of blood with alcohol, to ultimately *become alcohol himself.* "Goes down easy, I can't deny it!" Melt away, disappear, and dissolve *completely* into everything that our conscience encounters, said Roman a few months after starting college, and I don't see, now that these words are flooding my brain, I really don't see why I would challenge them—in fact I could very well have spoken them myself, all of them, and from way back. Roman often told me that his desire to dissolve completely into what his conscious mind encountered started manifesting itself early on, at six or eight years of age. It started with television, said Roman, or more accurately, at the time I came to understand that the various characters moving across my screen actually existed, so that they were not mere cartoons but characters subjected to the laws of an almost tangible physical reality, in any case a discernible and autonomous reality. Dissolve into television: this is the kind of idea, the kind of plan that I dreamt up at the age of six or eight, or thereabouts; first completely dissolve into television, then, the next logical step, become television myself. But obviously this nebulous agenda of mine had no chance of succeeding, and the more I watched television, the more I focused on watching it, the more I realized that this nebulous agenda, dreamt up by me somewhere around the age of six or eight, never got beyond the wishful thinking stage. I would sit and stare at the TV screen for hours at a time, having not the slightest notion of what I was watching, for hours on end I would virtually drown in it, almost completely, but never to the point of being able to entirely ignore the irreducible physical distance separating me from the screen. As soon as I was home alone, I ran over to the TV and turned it on: at first I would settle into an armchair about three yards from the set, then would move closer until I was, at most, ten inches from the screen. But it became obvious that my determination was getting me nowhere, and there was always, would always be, this very fine yet very solid and absolutely irreducible physical distance, barely one or two millimeters in reality, between my head and the screen. I repeated this same ritual for weeks without the slightest variation and whenever I was alone in the house, I went at it, and I even went at it so hard, so desperate was I to melt entirely into the screen that my nose and forehead were physically bruised. It was only after these hard few weeks of pig-headed determination—four or five, or thereabouts—that I finally realized that I could never *definitively* dissolve myself into my television, that I would never be able to absorb even just a piece of this physical reality external to my consciousness and that never again would I be able to even momentarily ignore the irreducible distance between my head and the screen. My body was in the way. My body was in the way, said Roman, and it's probably this small, almost negligible surplus, no more than 150–200 lbs. on average, that prevents us from renouncing ourselves for good, and that, in all circumstances, prevents us from completely dissolving into what our consciousness collides with. I wasn't ready to give up just yet, said Roman, but the more my mind sought to invest in all the dimensions of an object, say a TV or a vase, the more my mind or my head sought to occupy the entire volume of this same object, the more that object, literally absorbed by my head or my mind, resisted my effort. I could stare at this object for several long minutes, meticulously observe it from every angle; I could grasp it with all my might for several minutes, applying greater and greater pressure; I could turn it every which way, flip it over or even crack it; I could finally let this same object break through and then invade the totality of my mind, and by that I mean, grant it the freedom to make use of all parts of my head: something like a body was resisting me. Something like *my* body was resisting *us.* We flit, bee-like, from one object to another, buzzing, gleaning and gathering our way, *almost* sucking out their marrow; but instead of dissolving there, rather than letting ourselves be completely absorbed by them, we *bump up* against our own body. We are constantly bumping up against our body and we constantly repeat the same operation and whenever our mind meets an object, our mind constantly bumps against our body. But I obviously couldn't abandon this project, nor could I bring myself to put down permanent roots in my mother—who had been methodically plotting my ruin since her birth. Now that I think of it, it's probably in order to escape the influence of motherly love, meaning to loosen the stranglehold that my head had been firmly fixed in for years, that it was so imperative that I find a way to dissolve myself somewhere—in a TV or a vase, let's say. Now that I think of it, if I persisted so doggedly in obliterating bit by bit the slightest distance that separates me from the objects that my mind or my head happen to seize upon, it was without a doubt, and I believe I can state this with near certainty at this point, to put down roots anywhere else but in my mother. Anywhere but there, said Roman. Naturally my mind never managed to completely disregard it, and naturally I was constantly bumping into something and naturally all of my attempts at complete dissolution always ended in dismal failure. Naturally. Naturally I also realized that this desire to disappear into each of the objects that my mind or my head was investing in, this urge cyclically aborted, annihilated and renewed over the course of several months, said Roman, this desire would one day or another reach its limit. But I couldn't reasonably give up on this project, and the television incident was only the beginning, said Roman, it was only the beginning of a very long series of attempts at dissolution each more unsuccessful than the last, an endless series of stinging defeats that I pathetically pursued, to the point of obsession. Roman told me a few weeks later (we were sitting in a lecture hall whose exact color escapes me after all these years; actually the color of this lecture hall, the special shade of the sky that day or even the particulars of what I was wearing have *absolutely* no significance), he told me that he never gave up on this project that he conceived more or less at the age of six or eight, and that however futile or sterile or even damaging it may have been, he has been relentlessly pursuing it all his life. I'll find a way someday, he said, to make this distance temporarily disappear, or better yet, to definitively eliminate this irreducible distance, this unbearable entity that separates my mind and the objects it latches onto. Without ever reaching this same obsessive and, finally, suicidal intensity behind Roman's urge to disappear into the objects that his mind or his head, as he said, would latch onto, I myself often catch my mind by surprise (I still catch it off guard today), first twirling around an object, then lingering for a moment around its forms, then entering straight into it. Although, as Roman said at the time, our mind's impulses inevitably collide with the inertia of our own bodies, this observation is childlike in its simplicity, but still, something goaded me to become one with various objects within my reach. Since our earliest childhood, I thought while observing the ungainly profile of my jolly toad of a travel companion, our mind is organized against our own body. As soon as we are vaguely aware of our body, in reality as soon as we begin to notice, and this form of lucidity develops very early in life, that our body is preventing us from mingling with and dissolving ourselves into the various objects within our reach, our mind begins conspiring. Since our earliest childhood our mind conspires to neutralize and demolish and overtake our body, and that's the truth. And this special way of conspiring, which, for example, pushes us from the age of four or five to play with dolls, or play cowboys and Indians, this early behavior is obviously called imagination. Imagining oneself as a cowboy, to dress in the perfect cowboy outfit, to get the cowboy look down to the smallest detail, in short, to dissolve into a cowboy at the age of four or five or six only reveals, finally, our will to rid ourselves of our body at the first opportunity. For both a child at a young age and an adult in full possession of his faculties, to imagine themselves as something other than what their body prescribes, to aspire to an elsewhere largely inaccessible to bodily inertia, to purposefully disregard their body, yes all of these impulses point to nothing else, basically, than their desire to die. The sooner the better. In each of these flights of imagination, I now thought while adjusting my synthetic blanket, each of these nonsensical escapades that our imagination engages—like that of dissolving into a television or a vase—there lurks a barely concealed desire for death, and ultimately the imagination, to which humanity supposedly owes its most splendid works of art and its most amazing scientific advances, well, imagination is but the mind's *deadly* rejoinder to the body. The mind's rejoinder to itself, in essence. The countless trips that our imagination is guilty of are each little self-administered deaths, and when all is said and done, our imagination serves only one purpose: to forever be ridding our minds of the body's unbearable reality. That is, to always die a little bit more. And this undoubtedly does us an enormous favor. "I'll have the same thing again, please." It was in those rare moments when I would escape the despicable *huis clos* that my mother had lovingly concocted at my birth and unfailingly maintained thanks to her inexhaustible imagination, that is, those rare moments when she begrudgingly gave me permission, in some incomprehensibly lax moment, to leave home to join up with the few friends I had managed to make, in those moments I realized how inclined my mind had become to *transform* itself into everything it encountered. Since I couldn't get rid of my body, or disappear completely into the objects that caught my gaze, though I felt sure I would someday make that happen, as they say, I had become a kind of sponge. As soon as I left my house, my mind would abandon my body; as soon as I crossed paths with a stranger on the street, my mind would tag along; as soon as I spoke to a neighbor, my spirit penetrated his every pore. I was transformed. I was transformed, said Roman, into something constantly unstable, into something whose final shape I couldn't begin to imagine, in any case. The first significant transformation, the one I remember most vividly, brings me back to my twelfth or thirteenth year, precisely at the time when my mother, who would normally never accept such deviations, needed to leave on a trip involving global business—and global business of course waits for no one. Just as one would drop off a dog at the kennel before leaving on summer vacation, my mother had entrusted me, for however long it would take to handle this global business of hers that not even a trifle such as war could impede, she entrusted me to a couple of friends who had children my age, twins. Perfectly identical twins, a wonder of nature, same hair, same face, same build, dressed exactly the same—the kind of twins that are guests on television talk shows. Perfectly identical except for one detail: the younger, by only a few seconds, had a horrible stutter. You had to wait several minutes for him to pronounce even the beginning of a word, a few more to hear two uninterrupted words in succession, and an extra five minutes to finally hear a sentence that was more or less coherent. As soon as he attempted to speak, you had to get ready to experience a long stretch of weariness, annoyance or astonishment. His thoughts were pretty near impenetrable, and no one could ever tell what he was getting at. With him nothing was simple, nothing was ever explicit: we lapsed most often into the unspoken, in fact we either lapsed into the utterly incomprehensible or we settled on the unspoken. I wonder even now whether the stuttering—which affected his whole family and everyone around him—was ruining his elocution alone or whether it was also damaging his thought process. Did he think in stutters, too? In any case, Clement, who was certainly not lacking in finesse or mischievousness, also developed other stuttering techniques for holding his audience spellbound; he knew, as they say, how to keep you hanging on. He had these techniques down to such a science, in fact, he was so skilled at applying them that, for example, he was able to start a sentence in his usual laboriously halting fashion, as would be expected from him, then he would suddenly speed up his pronunciation with such fluency that for several seconds, his listeners, so devilishly hoodwinked, would believe that his initial stuttering had been totally simulated. Clement had this stunning way of alternating between stretches of simulation and stretches of authentic stuttering; Clement sowed doubt in our minds; but Clement would still invariably fall back into his agonizing impairment. But I have to admit he was a grand master, said Roman. A real one-of-a-kinder, in a class all his own, *a standout.* Needless to say this one-week stay in the kennel only served to confirm this very peculiar mental disposition of mine to turn myself into everything I observe, short of, completely dissolving into the object of my observation. The sponge that I had gradually become could hardly have dreamt up a specimen as phenomenal as Clement, it could not pass up the unique opportunity to distinguish itself in turn, which is why it seemed unthinkable to me not to appropriate what made him such a *standout*: his stutter. Scarcely had my mother returned from her global business trip, and thus scarcely had I been recommitted to the stifling confines of my *huis clos* than I started to stutter as well. I started to stutter and stammer, said Roman that day, and not a single syllable, not a word or sentence left my mouth that wasn't lavishly manhandled, tortured, and trampled by my stutter. The more I trained, the more I mastered these diverse pronunciation techniques that Clement displayed with such uncanny ease, in short, the more diligently I practiced every manner of stuttering, the less my mind, literally trained, felt it had to be conscious of the stuttering that it produced. I stuttered automatically, better and better, *without thinking about it.* Did I think in a stutter? I can't remember anymore. But after a week my whole being had gotten into the habit and stuttering had become *almost* natural, so to speak. Not only had the stutter become *almost* natural, not only had this stutter ceased to consult with my mind or my mouth in order to thrive, but in addition, I realized that Clement, to whom I owe this radical experiment, had vanished from my mind. I stuttered automatically, with increasing proficiency, without thinking about it—without thinking about Clement. In reality, the more I perfected my stutter, said Roman, the higher its degree of complexity, *thus*, the *closer* my stutter approached the virtuosity of Clement's, and the less I was actually thinking about Clement. Somewhere along the way I had simply put Clement out of my mind and never again, not even once to be exact, did I think of him. Clement had instigated my own stutter; Clement even graciously served as the exclusive model, but somewhere along the way, at a moment I'm not able to pinpoint, Clement was, very naturally and effortlessly, put out of my mind. And in putting this poor Clement out my mind, in misplacing him somewhere along the way, I spirited away his stutter—his standout trait—I virtually drained him of his substance. I had, in the end, simply wiped him out. "The same thing. With a little less tonic." Despite the immense irritation of my mother, who would stoop to just about anything, including immediately sending me to consult a professional, as they say in polite circles, in order to muzzle my behavioral fantasies, despite this immense irritation, as I said, the stuttering episode, which lasted barely seven or eight weeks, this episode revealed to me how my mind or my head was capable of turning into whatever it encountered. My mother could no longer fight it, despite all her self-interested concern and her abhorrent retaliation measures, (at the time when he was unloading all this on me—and my version is but a pale approximation—Roman used an expression in connection with all of these retaliation measures that he was subjected to, and the expression was "chemical straightjacket." To put an end to my stuttering, my mother had ever so logically and without hesitation decided to have me silenced, he said) she could no longer fight and it seems to me now that I think of it that not a week went by without me turning completely into something else or rather, into someone else. It's very simple, said Roman, as soon as I noticed a distinctive sign, any sign of singularity or personal peculiarity, as soon as my eyes lingered a little longer than usual on this or that feature I've always felt I was *essentially* lacking, my mind laid claim to it. Here's how it worked: first my mind would more or less consciously appropriate the new trait, then it would turn itself *almost* completely into what it had assimilated. My ability to transform myself *almost* completely reached such levels of diversification that within a few months I had managed, almost effortlessly, to change how I walk three or four times, how I gesticulate five or six times,—not to mention the countless transformations in my facial expressions and diction techniques, or even in my dress. All it took was even the most fleeting exposure to an environment, or a situation where I was facing another person, for my mind to instantly put down roots, for my mind to appropriate that person's distinctive signs and for my mind, ultimately, to *almost* turn into him. My head had become a sponge and everything that my mind encountered, everything that my mind soaked up, everything that my mind turned into constituted a kind of tentative and incomplete repudiation in my body. Stuttering, changing my posture or displaying a funny new walk signified nothing less, Roman said that day, than a repudiation of my body, than an *imperfect* and twisted way to punish it, above all, a way to imprint it with unnatural patterns and physical distortions. But all of this, all of these transformations instigated by my mind, however numerous and varied and amazing, never definitively rid me of my body. They could certainly redress this body; they could momentarily inflict this or that quirk; but never to the point of eradicating it completely. Try as it might to transform itself almost completely into everything it encountered, to pilfer everyone else's marks of distinction whether basic features or deeply personal traits, to properly assimilate all of this, my body kept up its resistance, my body resisted time and again. I developed almost the same gait as Karl's or Lucas's, I appropriated almost exactly the same facial expressions as Georges's, the same laugh as Philippe's; but there was always this excruciating *almost* that constantly intervened between intention and perfection, in reality an extraordinarily excruciating *almost* that constantly taunted and blocked me on the road to perfection—*almost* complete, *almost* perfect, *almost* natural. Almost. "Wake me up in twenty minutes." As it turned out, my body was clearly not the only one resisting. Actually, my head and my body banded together so that I could never arrive at completely, perfectly, and definitively transforming myself into what my mind encountered. How to explain my nearly complete and almost perfect transformation, in other words, my structural incompetence and my pathetic failures, indeed, how to explain these repeated failures if not by the ruthless coalition of my head and my body. Roman told me that day that he was virtually always just a heartbeat away from perfectly transforming himself and then disappearing completely, always just a heartbeat away from finishing off both mind and body: a heartbeat away from becoming something else. *But I still looked a little too much like myself,* he said, I probably looked a little too much like myself, and I have been, start to finish, only a copy of an original—a copy, for example, of Clement, a copy of Karl or Lucas or Georges. A more or less faithful copy, a more or less perfect copy; but a copy nonetheless. And yet, from all of these more or less conscious transformations, I naturally believed the result couldn't possibly be a copy, not some shabby, pathetic, ridiculous facsimile, what would inevitably be a degenerate reproduction of an original, but instead I was sure I'd become an actual original, a duplicate, *an original beside an original.* Like twins. But somewhere along the way my head and body banded together, they joined forces to ensure that all my attempts would end in failure, that they would always end, as the expression goes, in a resounding defeat. That day (it was a Wednesday if I remember correctly), Roman concluded that he was doomed to be nothing more than *a copy beside an original,* only a nasty defect next to absolute perfection, he said that he would never be able, as he had once so ardently desired, to pride himself on being an original beside an original. And, for that matter, he continued, I realized that the more my mind glimpsed perfection, the more perfection escaped me, or to put it another way, I realized that the more my mind effectively drew closer to the original, the more the irreducible gap that separated us widened. In the end, I was a kind of fake, a forgery, an *almost,* and that's the truth. A residue of something infinitely meaningless. Most likely a residue of individuality. Almost nothing, you might just as well say. So I looked like nothing—except my father, it seems (Roman never discussed the man at any length, the one his mother Johanna referred to as the cowardly bastard who had abandoned his own in a trice; only a few sporadic references to the city of Wuppertal, some allusions here and there, a few hazy remarks disingenuously inserted at the end of a sentence and whose meaning remained an impenetrable enigma for anyone who didn't have the privilege of attending Roman's endless rants. In short, nothing of substance, and even his relatively close acquaintances never got anything but random bits of information on this particular subject. But oddly enough, I thought now while turning off the overhead light, oddly enough Roman hadn't seemed to hesitate one bit, the third or fourth time we met, to tell me about his trip to Wuppertal. I'm planning a trip to Wuppertal in the very near future, he confided on the evening of our fourth meeting, I've found out that my father's on his deathbed, which is why I absolutely have to get to Wuppertal, before he kicks the bucket. I have to make it to Wuppertal or bust. Of course, his mother Johanna took a dim view of this trip to Wuppertal, she with her grand design, he said that night, she who had methodically plotted out my life down to the slightest detail to get him out of the picture only a few months after my birth, she who never mentioned his name without associating it with as much vile innuendo and slander as she could, defiling whatever vague memory I might have kept of him, this woman, with her lifetime devotion to the crassest and most extraordinarily base stupidity, this woman doubtless too subhuman to merit the name of woman, this woman that fate has assigned as my unspeakably lame progenitor, she got it into her head that I simply shouldn't go to Wuppertal and that my father's supposedly fatal disease was nothing more than a ruse, and finally, that this whole Wuppertal business was nothing but a crude trap, and that Wuppertal, the *armpit of the Ruhr,* in her words, has earned the dubious honor of being the ugliest, most repulsive city in all of Germany. It took me three months to scrape together enough money for the trip, Roman told me after his return from Wuppertal, so I had to wait three months to get to the bedside of a man I knew to be deathly ill, which amounted to exactly one week after the illness had done him in, exactly one week *after.* One week after his death and just hours before the funeral service, I arrived in Wuppertal, as it happens I got there just in time for the burial in the rain and in the midst of a sizable gathering of strange faces; I was told here is your family, here is your father's coffin. In a cemetery on the outskirts of Wuppertal I was planted amidst a sizable gathering of strangers pretending to give a damn and then telling me here is your German family, your German grandmother and cousins; here is the coffin of your German father. I was planted in the middle of my German family and then I was told we're going to take you in, I was told *to speak* one last time to my father who had lost his battle with illness. Under a white tent on the outskirts of Wuppertal, said Roman, two or three days after his return, somewhere in the Ruhr, I found myself face to face with the coffin of my father, carried away by a deadly disease, and I thought to myself, finally alone with the coffin, that *this most likely cold and stinking corpse could not be my father's*, I told myself that even though the corpse, probably cold and stinking, was indeed my father's, which I am perfectly willing to concede since they insisted several times that it was so, I could not talk to him, I thought, still facing the coffin, I just couldn't talk to him—even if it was indeed the corpse of my father—*because I can't speak German.* It was only in a huge cemetery on the outskirts of Wuppertal, in the rain, among some one hundred Germans, and face to face with my German father that I realized the full extent to which I couldn't speak German—*the language of my father*—and wouldn't you know that at the very moment it was absolutely imperative that I speak German, that I realized how utterly foreign German was to me. Under a white tent and wedged onto a wooden chair and surrounded by members of my German family I heard the speeches and tributes in German that I couldn't grasp, speeches they had to translate for me several hours later, speeches and tributes that they must have had to fabricate. In the middle of the funeral procession, after a winding path on the edge of a clearing, I understood that my grief could be nothing but *the product of a fabrication*, a few meters from the family vault in the Wuppertal cemetery I realized that an *insurmountable language barrier*—the language of my father—prohibited me from acknowledging that this cold and stinking corpse was my father, and surrounded by members of my German family, watching the coffin being lowered into the earth, I understood above all that no filial connection would be possible with this cold and stinking corpse that we were now leaving to the mercy of the elements. Standing before the tombstone and among my family, I was subjected to the infinitely contrite face of the German Catholic priest and to the *sincere* condolences of the others—all Germans—*and it is quite obviously when people—especially Germans—attempt to comfort us that we are utterly destroyed.* In an outpouring of abject sincerity and compassion under a huge chestnut tree, people were falling over each other to finish off my destruction, on that second of June, terribly aggrieved, one after another they rushed to shake my hand, to fondle my face in the rain, signifying to me in English how much I resembled, down to the last feature, my German father. Later in the afternoon, in a restaurant near the Wuppertal cemetery, people in still relatively large numbers started up all over again, a concerting throng of them—they were Germans, after all—joined forces to drive the nail in a little deeper and tell me, one after the other, *how everything about me, my gestures, my gait, my facial expressions, my smile, reminded them of my father.* It's amazing, they said innocently, it's simply amazing how much you look like him even though nothing about you, your gait, your expressions, your smile, which are all exactly identical to those of your father, could result from any kind of *mimicry*, since you never knew him. On the flight back from Wuppertal, despite the annoying person in the seat next to mine, I spent a long while rehashing what everyone had so offhandedly affirmed to me in the cemetery on June second, and I thought, after careful consideration, that all my life I have been literally imitating someone I didn't know, and while I was at it, I thought that maybe I had marshaled everything to *resemble to a tee a dead person.* Thus, on June second, the Germans plunged me into the family vault next to the cold, stinking corpse of my father). I didn't resemble anything, said Roman, except my father, it would seem; I was still only a heartbeat away from complete transformation and I was forever nestled into this tiny space that separates the idea from its execution and kept bumping up against the coalition of my body and my head. But now that I'm analyzing the phenomenon in hindsight, that is, after having lived through it, and with a brain a bit more developed than at the time, I think that these almost complete transformations enacted by my mind and imperfectly imposed upon my still recalcitrant body, that these changes took place perhaps outside of any conscious process per se. In reality, we wouldn't say hey what if I were to develop a tic, then suddenly I start having a tic—and so on. You can't just prescribe things so straightforwardly, so unimaginatively, idiotically. Analyzing the phenomenon with my brain today and after having actually lived through it all, I know that things can never be summed up in terms of a maneuver as predictable as one consisting of first formulating a goal, then comfortably achieving it; with my brain as it is today, I now know this, at the very least. With the benefit of hindsight, and upon closer inspection, I can now reasonably argue that after a while my head no longer perceived or identified the distinctive signs it appropriated, quite the contrary. It's just the opposite, said Roman, and I'm quite sure that apart from this stuttering episode, which involved a more or less conscious acquisition, apart from this founding episode of all of my transformations, as faithful to their original model as they were, they had to do with *involuntary imitation.* Unlike imitation professionals, whose practice consists only of providing temporary lodging to the thing they imitate, with the main purpose of getting laughs, we might say—since the whole idea should *always* be about laughs, about caricature, shouldn't it?—in these circumstances and within a precise timeframe, unlike those who *occasionally change their mask but always keep the same face,* for my part, I never imitated willfully and with specific goals in mind, I didn't change my mask on command, as they say, for money or to impress folks, in reality *I never changed masks but involuntarily changed faces.* Back then, which I can now analyze with the intellectual tools available to me today, it was impossible for me to target those whose substance I would drain so imperfectly, just as it was impossible for me to voluntarily imitate them and to deploy that kind of mental pliability that professional imitators are gifted with. At the time, I would simply fall into alignment. At the time I would systematically and indiscriminately align myself with everything that my mind encountered, said Roman, I think at the time I never voluntarily appropriated Karl's gait or Georges's facial expressions or Philippe's laugh, that kind of prowess belonged only to imitation professionals, but *I woke up one morning, so to speak, with Karl's gait and Georges's facial expressions and Philippe's laugh.* Overnight, and without even trying, I found I was walking almost exactly like Karl, that I'd borrowed Georges's facial expressions and that my laugh sounded an awful lot like Philippe's. From one day to the next, I woke up with a new face—involuntarily and for who knew how long—that was Karl's, Georges's or Philippe's. I was placed in a certain setting, and it was only the next day that I realized how much I had been imitating everyone in this setting. I simply aligned myself and did so unconsciously, an overnight discovery that I had aligned myself to this or that person, totally unaware of when the alignment had kicked in. And when you take this alignment all the way, though unintentionally, when you discover after the fact that you had indeed imitated Georges or Karl or Philippe, well I think that it is precisely these others, Karl Georges Philippe, who after a while start to walk or wince or laugh inside your body, instead of you; I think ultimately, when aligned so spontaneously and in complete unawareness, with everything that your mind is encountering, that *it's the others who are positively swarming within you, the others who squat in both your mind and body, where they proliferate and take control.* Analyzing the phenomenon today I can state with certainty that I was *inhabited* and bullied and manhandled by everyone my mind encountered, and with equal certainty that my head and my body were impounded and turned over to Karl Phillipe Georges and to anyone else they might imitate, and finally, I am just as certain that by stealing their distinctive signs they were not emptied of their substance, it wasn't me who annihilated them: it was them. They were the ones who destroyed me, said Roman, whoever they may be, they were the ones who destroyed me and who are destroying me still: because *from now on I owe them everything.* From that point forward, I've been unable to claim any of my distinctive features, any of my personal qualities, any marks of distinction, and now none of my behaviors, and what's worse, *none of my thoughts*, can overcome this feeling of *permanent debt*, which means that I am immediately suspicious of where my behaviors and thoughts are coming from, immediately inclined to purge them of any suspicion of involuntary imitation. Far more than my grins or my various physical behaviors, it's my thoughts—my opinions, my views, my conversation—that can't overcome the feeling of permanent debt, it's my thoughts, absolutely all my thoughts, said Roman, that have been taken away from me to be *given back* to the others. The fact that I can occasionally, and by all rights, lay claim to any particular thought—an entirely plausible accident, mind you—the fact that, in all humility I can claim the paternity of a particular statement, is of absolutely no importance, *since now it's the overall economy of my thoughts that has been placed under the supervision of others.* You need only wake up once or twice with someone else's thoughts or words in your head, you need only catch yourself once or twice uttering words, phrases, or arguments that clearly belong to Karl Georges Phillipe to feel invalidated, or fraudulent or outright *dispossessed of* your entire stock of words, phrases, and arguments—involuntary imitation is essentially limitless. "It's funny how twenty minutes of rest really perks a guy up. You'll have some coffee with me, won't you? Let me ring for the stewardess." On my way to the toilets, still irritated by the predictably tedious and trivial conversation with my seatmate Biroult (his name just came back to me), I overheard some passengers using the language of my so-called homeland, that filthy cesspool that I was never supposed to return to, and which will undoubtedly start asphyxiating me as soon as I set foot on the tarmac. Both passengers—impeccably dressed—looked terribly smug and self-satisfied to be gossiping so viciously without being understood by their target, the flight attendant (who was, admittedly, a bit clumsy). Without noticing me, these two passengers had, in a way that was probably more violent than Roman's more gradual resurfacing in my consciousness after many years of suppression, brought back an era, a language, and a country that I've been trying desperately to dislodge. All it took was a few sentences uttered in my so-called native language for these two passengers—in their ostentatiously expensive shoes—to demolish years of effort, I thought as I dried my hands in the foul-smelling aircraft toilet, barely two or three insults casually tossed out by these vulgar oafs—they were still carrying on about the flight attendant—and those years and years of hard work were destroyed in a flash. Exiting the toilet, my eyes meeting theirs only furtively, the two passengers saw fit to aim a couple of their barbs at me—some childish jab about my glasses—still believing that I couldn't understand anything they were saying. Returning to my seat, I thought that I would have greatly preferred not to understand their catty remarks about my glasses, I thought that more than anything else in the world, I would have liked not to understand a single word of anything they said: because those words pointed to my definitive confinement in a language, in a country, and in a past that was beyond repulsive. We move stubbornly forward, we acquire a new language, we divest ourselves of the past, and then we are sucked back to square one, stuck once again in that past. Despite years of estrangement and despite the lack of practice and despite all my best efforts, I understood every word, alas: I still had what it took, as the quip goes, and nothing they could say escaped the fluency that I continued—against all odds—to exercise with regard to this language. Against all odds, I persisted in understanding a language that I not only had ceased to speak for over ten, twelve years but that I had also tried desperately and methodically to cast out of my brain. For ten years I battled the odds to kill the polyglot in me, in reality it's taken more than twelve years to be precise for me to almost rid myself of this highly destructive trilingualism (my so-called mother tongue) that had infested my mind very early on, and that kept me from thinking straight for such a long time. I would have probably never managed to think properly with three languages constantly competing in my mind, I thought while sipping my first drop of soda, to try and think simultaneously in three languages was simply tantamount to the death of thought, because a thought, however shallow, is never built over a linguistic abyss, over a void, in other words. I now know that if I had not undertaken this draconian program of linguistic cleansing, if this cleansing policy had not borne a modicum of fruit, meaning a modicum of rightness in the construction and in the expression of some basic reasoning or other, I would have never been able to predict any result other than a total collapse of my thought process. To save my thoughts from complete collapse it was imperative that I rid myself of the inaccuracies inherent in my so-called mother tongue, that I neutralize this altogether *paralyzing* static that it inflicted on my brain, that I finally overcome the state of blatant intellectual *helplessness* where my so-called mother tongue detained me for so long, preying upon my mental health. With a sort of perfectly criminal inconsistency, people are persistently amazed at natural trilingualism, and regard any simultaneous practice of foreign languages, any mastery of various linguistic cultures with naïve admiration; they will always detect in this so-called virtuosity a sign of intellectual wealth that is sublime and admirable and enviable, and of course that's not how it is at all. That's not how it is at all, of course it isn't, so by and large, this apparent linguistic richness does nothing but encourage the erecting of a veritable *Tower of Babel in the brain* and frankly speaking, all this virtuosity in the use of languages amounts to something more akin to *linguistic schizophrenia.* What language do the virtuosos of natural trilingualism dream in, I wonder; which one do they think in, in which language are they capable of expressing themselves from start to finish without switching—they themselves don't even know, which is why I've kept at it for over twelve years, to not only eradicate all the toxic effects that my so-called mother tongue generates—inaccuracy, impotence, speech paralysis —but also to completely purge my brain of this mutant mongrel of a three-headed language. As soon as I'd unpacked my bags (it was the month of June), I immediately took up the challenge, come hell or high water, of eradicating any trace of this mutant mongrel that was eating away at my brain, even if it meant people might call me ungrateful, and despite the resistance that my kind of linguistic conservatism aroused, I was suddenly trying desperately, resolutely, to stop speaking, to stop thinking, to stop dreaming in my native language which—and this is its eradicable sin—is somehow never really there in the first place. Once my bags were unpacked, I could assess the extent of the damage as they say, I came to realize that I wasn't speaking in any one language in particular—especially not the one that I'm currently thinking in—and there came a time when I was no longer capable of even completing a sentence. All that juggling of languages had reduced me to silence, I was somehow dwelling in a very special place where the overabundance of languages turned, strangely into empty space, a space of *technical unspeakability.* "One thing I can say for sure is that . . ." But in reality nothing has been more perilous, I thought while letting my annoying Biroult pass, nothing has been more fraught than the correction of this formidable linguistic defect: *the left-handed must become right-handed*, that's all there was to it. It took years of toil, sometimes superhuman effort, and much disillusionment along the way. To become right-handed took years and years of hard work during which, seen from one perspective, I labored to expel this linguistic tumor—because that's exactly what all this impotence amounted to—a linguistic tumor that would be requiring emergency surgery; but from another perspective, I kept banging against this impregnable *fortress* that consists of acquiring a *partially* new language—meaning a language that you first have to forget and then learn again from scratch. "Excuse me, sorry." Native speakers question their own language situation in a far too anecdotal fashion, I thought now as I got up to let him by again, they only too rarely wonder about the exact nature of the linguistic dungeon that they've been locked into; they've been formatted to the extreme from day one and can't even see it anymore; they think and talk and chat away but know nothing of the terms of their confinement, they are simply content, especially the best educated of course, to marvel and enjoy and offhandedly, snootily jeer at the ubiquity of some cliché, some stock expression or platitude. Ah, what a cliché, they say smugly. These people, the most outrageously educated, imagine themselves living their own lives in some cliché-free zone—far from the cliché-ridden commoners. They move about at these supposedly privileged latitudes, believing they are resisting the lure of cliché without ever resorting to it themselves, *and in doing so, actually reside outside their language.* And yet once you enter into a language, you realize that nothing escapes the infinite empire of the cliché—whence the notion of imprisonment—and, it goes without saying, that language is primarily a matter of clichés. It's even the very backbone, the core of its communicability. Once you set your mind to acquiring it as perfectly as a native speaker, a goal I rather fanatically set for myself a little more than twelve years ago, you are all the more aware of how much a language is intelligible, assimilable and practicable only to the extent that it abounds in these much-maligned clichés, in other words, that it abounds in the thoughts, metaphors, and expressions, *ludicrous but often unsurpassable* that past generations have articulated, enriched, refined and transmitted well ahead of us. I eventually came to admit, now that this new language was almost perfectly grafted onto my brain, it was now possible for me to confess—for someone who was anxious to learn everything from scratch—how the general utility value of cliché could justify (and no doubt continue to justify even today) these poignant stirrings of pride that I would experience every time I had the privilege of hearing, understanding, and reproducing a platitude. You enter into a language the way you enter into prison, I thought to myself now, and in my case I entered head-first, gleefully into a language, but then suddenly became aware of how prison-like this language felt, where escaping the clutches of cliché is quixotic at best, and where at the end of the day it is impossible to *have a word of one's own.* But it would appear that despite all my best efforts and all the obstacles I continue to face and all my idle speculation about language, it would appear that I was somehow fated for this collapse of my thought process, that the prospect was at least *dangled before me,* since I seemed somehow determined to understand every word that these two passengers in the rear of the cabin were using just now, I thought as I re-adjusted my synthetic blanket, that by spouting with such impunity their petty little insults in a language I had promised to dislodge from my head and alas whose subtleties I still knew, these two passengers—clearly the unsavory offspring of former gang leaders ennobled by the bounty of war—these passengers represented, without even realizing it, the living proof of my most inescapable failure. "How about something else to drink?" Roman didn't have what I still considered as the good fortune, he never had the good fortune to leave his country and his language behind, even though he perceived, probably better than anyone, the absolutely lethal danger involved in residing within this kind of spiritual, intellectual, and linguistic *garbage dump* that pretends to be a country. Yet it's largely thanks to him that I feel almost in the clear now, it's largely thanks to Roman that, though I'm undoubtedly still facing considerable challenges, such as how to escape the clutches of cliché or how to slow down the rate of failure, but in the aggregate, these are less immediately perilous than his own. In all modesty, I think I'm out of the woods, while Roman is probably still struggling to this day, mired in the muck of natural trilingualism. As long as I stick around here I'll never get anywhere, he said back then. As long as I stay in this *languageless country* where most of my mental activity and all my intellectual effort consist of finding a way to string together a complete sentence in one and the same language, as long as I'm literally straightjacketed in my so-called mother tongue—*the language of my mother*—let's face it, I'm a lost cause. It's very simple, he said, shortly before my departure, either I leave this language or I resign myself to the degradation that's in store for me. Even though I'm retelling all this with my current words and syntax, neither of which have almost *anything in common* with my words and syntax of the time, I still have a very clear memory of that sentence—uttered one Saturday night over a bottle of rotgut red. We were in a sort of tavern that served as headquarters, ground zero you might say, for a loose community of greasy-haired poets, we were in this rather enchanted place, when Roman admitted to me that despite his best efforts—Herculean, as he said—to dislodge this so-called language of origin from his head, in short these Herculean efforts to *legitimately* feel like a perfect stranger in his own country, something like an irremediable linguistic inertia—a ball and chain, in fact—kept him from going forward. As soon as I became aware of the lethal nature of my native language—the language of my mother—I immediately stopped using it, more or less successfully; and while I was at it, I even gave up any academic teachings that might foster its development (a decision whose usefulness I couldn't yet see at the time). From the age of eighteen or nineteen onward, I was entirely devoted to a single language, much to the chagrin of my mother and my classmates and my teachers, who viewed this switch as a kind of elitist, artificial, even kitschy refinement, to their great chagrin I stopped thinking, speaking or reading in anything except French. Long before he addressed this whole issue with me, and in such detail—or was it around the same time?—I myself noted the *frenzied rate* at which Roman was devouring books, and how his willingness to throw himself into French, as he said, bordered on obsession. I seem to recall that all of this started during a period when the war had reached its absolute pitch of lethal intensity, during a period where, among other priorities, one of the uppermost was to not die of boredom during long sieges of sometimes three or four consecutive weeks spent in underground tunnels. While my companions in misfortune were busy playing tarot or backgammon beneath the bombs, I lost myself in books, he said. This obsession with reading, according to the account that he gave me after the fact, this obsession earned him all manner of nasty sarcasm, since in this country of philistines who worship at the altar of crassness, reading, and in French no less, was akin to a kind of intolerable sickness that had to be carefully weeded out. The alternative, for example, was to become a tarot freak. But Roman didn't give an inch, as they say, quite the contrary, his obsession seemed to virtually thrive on all of the lame digs lobbed in his direction. It began during the darkest hours of the war and continued well beyond, every day Roman dove into French *the way you would dive into the body of a woman,* that is, greedily, eagerly, and awkwardly, it goes without saying. He read and read and read some more, in original version French texts. Everything he could get his hands on in French, newspapers, cookbooks, novels, gradually it was mostly novels, it seems, he read them indiscriminately. From the day we met until the eve of my departure, I never saw Roman without him lugging around one of those doorstop French novels that he procured from who knows where. I'm reading Rabelais or I'm reading Balzac or Flaubert or Proust, he would say. In fact, he read these authors so assiduously that he started talking very much like they did in the books, which is to say: artificially, often bombastically, and in any case, rarely *personally.* The more he read in a language that was, let's admit, unnatural, the more Roman was speaking someone else's French, those authors he read over and over; but it was French, and that seemed to be all that mattered. "Please fasten your seatbelts, we're going to be experiencing some turbulence." I ditched it all, Roman told me that evening of the dubious red wine in the downtown dive, I ditched my mongrel vocabulary, my mongrel syntax, and my mongrel expressions: all in favor of French. Of course, my immediate environment required that I frequently resort to my mother tongue, if only to communicate my needs and requests to the outside world, I had to give in. But that hardly mattered. Though the reasons for caving to my native language were still much more varied than I'd like to admit. It didn't take much. A momentary lapse of attention, for example. A *carelessness*, that's it, it took only a moment of carelessness to destroy everything, said Roman, and we are naturally never safe from carelessness of any sort, and it's this *reprehensible* carelessness that's the root of all of our ills and the guarantee of our structural impotence. All it takes is a little carelessness and we slink unceremoniously back to square one, doomed to start all over, from the beginning and in French.

Obstinate as I was, the edifice was so fragile that it took hardly anything to bring the whole thing crashing down, in spite of my hours and hours of reading, a trifle, call it an innocent little bit of carelessness, a mere soupçon would have me redoubling my effort, starting from the top. In truth, the more I caught myself involuntarily speaking my native language, the more I would dive into French; likewise, the more I threw myself into French, the more I caught myself using my native language. I was getting interference from both sides, in other words. One foot in each language and my head in a vise grip. "You don't seem like the *talkative* type. But hey, I haven't asked you yet: what is it you do, exactly?" This guy isn't going to give me even a moment's peace, is he? Interrupting my train of thought. Annoying the hell out of me, asking me all these trivial questions. Ever since I accepted to share some coffee—I never should have done that—this tiresome Biroult has seemed increasingly eager to start up the (one-way) conversation I thought we had clearly concluded only minutes ago. This type of person watches for any chink in the armor, and I saw him coming, Biroult, they take advantage of the smallest breach to break through and *settle* into us: *they make themselves at home.* With the intention of delving deeper. How many times have I been cornered like this, and by far less clever than Biroult. They would ask me have you got the time, or have you got change for coffee or have you got a light, and then they immediately dump their life story on your head. Some people are just waiting for the chance to dump their life story on your head, they don't care how, and no matter how underhanded their technique, the end result of a conversation remains the same: to dump their life story on your head. We're nothing but *an unanticipated excuse*, and there's something infuriating about that, I think. What more could we say, Biroult and I, and what good would it do. We've already said what needed to be said, it seems. Said about Biroult, that is. He laid it all out in fifteen minutes, which is already too much to summarize a life, since they all look the same. "Hey, you wouldn't happen to have something light to read, like a magazine, would you?" Awareness of his reprehensible carelessness had not yet discouraged Roman from stepping up his efforts, I thought while trying to resume the frayed thread of my thoughts, even though resorting to his native language was a harsh reminder, in his own words, of his definitive imprisonment in his native language, Roman never ceased to read and to read in original French. Although the quality of his intelligence prevented him from advancing *positively* toward a goal that he knew was, by nature, inaccessible, that is, to defeat his natural trilingualism, Roman literally strained to renounce any form of complacency or compromise with his native language. Escape through reading was the only—albeit imperfect—way that I had found to end my confinement, however tentatively and unconvincingly, he said. The only time I would escape the deadly inertia of my mother tongue, whose insistent *racket* and unholy screeching assaulted my brain from all sides, were the moments—ephemeral, he insisted—when I lost myself in books, or more precisely, within the purity of a single language, French. My cerebral activity fluctuated constantly between the fragile peace of my reading time and the inescapable annoyance that swept over me whenever I would hear the buzzing of my native language swarming within me, Roman said, while attacks from the outside left my brain open, so to speak, to the merciless onslaught of my native language, the one spoken daily in my immediate surroundings. I found a certain kind of miraculous respite—a lullaby of sorts—in the reading of Rabelais, Stendhal, Flaubert or Proust. To see and hear and even understand a succession of words in one language provided me with a totally new sense of harmony, something I had never experienced, an altogether new sensation that at least had the merit of interrupting, even if only temporarily, this kind of diffuse and steady roar, this extremely unpleasant background noise, to be more precise, that my daily language environment produced. However, the feeling of harmony that we procure from the *spectacle of reading* also starts to degrade, said Roman that evening, after several months of reading in French I realized that this spectacle of reading, initially so pleasant and indispensable, actually had turned against me: not only did this spectacle fail to extend into the linguistic reality that I faced daily, quite the opposite was true, because it pitted a model of unaffordable harmony against a desperate reality; not only did this spectacle of perfection provide the incontrovertible proof that I would never be able to make *a mother tongue out of a borrowed language*—the survival of my stubborn, mongrel trilingualism attested irrefutably to this failure—but I owed this observation to the increased attention I was starting to pay to what was actually *written* in Proust or Stendhal or Flaubert, and I also discovered, to my horror, that it meant I had landed *a bit too late* in this borrowed language, which I yearned to master, whatever the cost. It was when I got genuinely interested in what the French in the text was actually trying to say, when I could step back from the mere spectacle and the mere sound of the printed words to more seriously grasp the full scope of what I was reading at the time, it was at this moment, said Roman, exactly at this moment that I more or less understood both the full extent and the dire consequences of never being able to make up for that lost time.

Throwing myself into French as I had for months on end, I gradually realized how wide the time gap had grown, widening at the same rate as my settling into French, a gap very unlikely to ever be closed. Every time I read a page of Balzac or Stendhal, another gap, which I obviously hadn't known existed, would become apparent to me, and by the time I'd finished a whole book of Balzac or Stendhal, I realized I not only was no further along in my learning, but that I had undoubtedly *regressed*: henceforth the slight initial gap had in the end grown into a huge chasm. But you can't make up for lost time, as they say, and my reading Proust or Balzac or even Maupassant, which I was forced to pursue as an escape from the wretched linguistic reality of this country, was taking an increasingly lethal turn, all things considered, there was nothing left for me to do but to look upon my reading as a kind of *prerequisite annihilation*. Roman told me that evening (it was shortly before my departure), that he had long hoped to take some liberties with respect to what he had read in Proust and Beckett and even Maupassant, he told me, but I'm not so sure about that, since these one-way conversations took place over twelve years ago, he told me that his reading of these authors in the original French amounted to a prerequisite annihilation, and had already *charted the territory of this language* that he had so mightily struggled to master and that, as a result, as far as he was concerned, to think or speak differently than in books would have been a feat of prodigious proportions. Each time I read a book, its author charted the territory of this language for me, said Roman, every time I read a book, whether authored by Balzac or Proust or even Maupassant, the likelihood of finding, in the midst of this vast charted territory, *a parcel of language that was still untapped*, receded further into the distance.

All these authors, however illustrious, deprived me of the very possibility of regarding language as something other than a preordained loss at a game whose rules I had no choice but to obey, and now that I think of it, they deprived me of the very notion of possibility, of the virtual, of the infinite. By staking out the language terrain for me, all of these remarkable authors had, so to speak, *foreclosed this language*, after having each in his own way contributed to precluding, bit by bit, the very possibility of thinking or speaking in an original, or at least somewhat personal way, these authors completely foreclosed the language, shut me out of it. Of course, he said, I didn't always express myself exclusively like a Flaubert, or a Proust, or a Beckett, (that used to happen only during the hours immediately following my reading one of their books), and I would hope that my language proclivity hadn't reached such absurd proportions, but it seems to me that I did express myself *all together and all at the same time* like a Flaubert, a Proust, and a Beckett. I thought or talked simultaneously, in other words, like a Flaubert *and* a Proust, *and* a Beckett, said Roman, and as soon as I was able to think or speak in that yearned for language it was *involuntarily* the words, syntax, and idioms of Flaubert and Proust and Beckett that sprang to mind. Simultaneously and randomly, these authors tumbled into my helpless head, with me unable to maintain any distance with regard to what they had written, and unless I realized it right away and put up some, it must be said, rather half-hearted resistance, rarely was I able to strike out on a path other than the one that they had plotted for me. *I had a finger in every pie*, said Roman, finally it seemed that I had a finger in absolutely every single pie, and composed my thoughts and phrases based on those, fragmented or mixed or even completely intact, of Beckett and Proust and everyone else I was reading at the time. "The Captain has turned off the fasten seat belt sign." Roman pursued his monologue the day after that infamous evening which we ended, as I recall, in an advanced state of inebriation, by pronouncing—as soon as we met up, I'm now sure of it—a phrase that was, to say the least, surprising, and whose effects he seemed to have prepared ahead of time: writers rip off our ideas, he said. He had hardly even sat down in his metal chair before telling me that morning, with a kind of uncharacteristic firmness, telling me verbatim that writers ripped off our ideas. I need only read one page of any writer to conclude that, however widely admired he may be for his creative vitality and his artistic radicalism, he was draining my brain for his material, for those lovely phrases that have been impressing people for centuries. Often these writers are so damn arrogant, said Roman while I was straining to concentrate despite my hangover, they are so damn arrogant that they rip off *word for word*, the most original and the most profound of our ideas. It's not our puny, stammering, half-baked intuitions that these great writers so arrogantly rip off—since we can't claim authorship of thoughts that we ourselves have yet to clearly state—but our most markedly arresting, our most positively personal ideas, the ones we forged with our own experiences and our own observations. Not content to further foreclose the language, and to trace paths for us that we have no choice but to follow, the writers, especially the dead ones that we rightly describe as geniuses, ripped off our ideas, systematically and page after page, and it's only the most pathetically self-important among us that rejoice and go forth to spread the news of this happy coincidence with their awestruck friends. Here's what the great writers do, said Roman while downing his espresso, whose taste he claimed he couldn't stand, for reasons I still can't imagine, particularly since he drank espressos at a dizzying rate, often ten per day or whenever he happened to feel tired, which was all the time, he would knock back ten or twelve a day, these writers rip off our most personal ideas and reduce us to silence and build their genius reputations on this original sin. These great writers live off an abject transgression that has reduced us to silence after having unrepentantly robbed us of all our ideas, and that's the truth, he said, plunking his coffee cup down on the right corner of the table. Naturally the more we admire the writer whose books we read with a perfectly idiotic devotion, the more this writer is ripping off our ideas, continued Roman, paying no heed at all to the sentence I was about to say, you've got to believe that the more we think we share affinities with a writer, the more this writer, so completely, so *irresponsibly* admired by us, rips off our ideas and ventriloquizes us, and we are consequently reduced to silence. A serendipitous and ingenuous *delegation of speech* is what the irresponsible reader believes upon discovering some affinity with the admired writer, when in reality it is indeed a systematic rip-off of his most personal ideas and a *definitive* stifling of his own speech. Every time we read a great writer and feel flattered when we notice that his ideas, viewpoints or general impressions sound exactly like ours, we are immediately *forced to relinquish our own speech.* As I woke up this morning, still pretty buzzed from last night's bender, Roman said unexpectedly that morning, I was standing in front of my bookshelves about to remove a tome—recommended by our friend Isabelle—one that I had kept putting off reading for reasons I couldn't explain until right now (something along the lines of a *bad vibe*, no doubt): *Die Ursache*, in my French edition, *L'Origine*, by Thomas Bernhard, a *German-language* writer (a copy of this book is currently sitting on my desk, which is to say, twelve years later). After casting a curious glance at the plot summary on the back cover, which referred to it as an *autobiographical* narrative, I opened the book with the intention of flipping through it quickly, when I landed *by chance* on page 50, from which I'll read you a very short paragraph: "Everyone, it seems, has lost the memory of those destroyed houses and people killed back then, everyone has forgotten or would rather not know." Utterly stunned, as I continue to flip through the book with a kind of nervousness that's hard to contain, there, again at random, on page 90. Here's an eloquent sample: "The new human being is always birthed by its mother like an animal, and forever treated like an animal." Absolutely terrified, I kept reading, flipping a few pages back, and landed, again at random, on this sentence on page 37, which apparently deals with populations bombed during the war: "They accepted the humiliation and the uninterrupted destruction of their being." Feeling an overpowering wave of nausea, said Roman, while drinking his second espresso, feeling an overpowering wave of nausea, and at this point fairly certain that a vomiting fit was imminent, I went ahead and read the whole book, *L'Origine*, in just over an hour and immediately phoned our friend Isabelle, only to hang up before she could answer, and ran to the bathroom to spill my guts. Gradually revived, I headed to my room and started digging through drawers in search of an old notebook I'd started a few weeks before the end of the war, where I'd written down my moods and thoughts of the moment. And here's what I produced back then, Roman said, handing me his old notebook, which he later gave me as a gift on the eve of my departure: "The carefree inhabitants of this city don't realize that today's streets where they so love to parade are nothing more than an enormous, smoldering cemetery." Several pages later, as the sun sank below the horizon, I also made out this sentence: "We'd learned to accept daily humiliation without batting an eye." After ordering another espresso, Roman fingered a passage—all the way at the end of the notebook—a paragraph written in a rather sloppy hand a bit difficult to decipher: "She brought me into this world (then something completely illegible) and then immediately shoved me into an inescapable Machiavellian trap." And this was just one example among others, Roman said that afternoon, these lines that were almost identical in meaning, even in their formal intention, are more than an innocent coincidence that I'm not so stupid as to take delight in, these few lines, Selber, are a rip-off, no two ways about it, of the ideas that I myself clearly laid down in this notebook five or six months ago. Once I'd finished reading Thomas Bernhard's *L'Origine,* I realized, frankly, in a morbid state of depression whose longevity I could already foresee, that a significant portion of my thoughts, observations, and analyses were expressed as such in a text that I had nevertheless not written. This Austrian writer's book was crammed with my own ideas, said Roman, so I might as well just give up and go home. "Sir, would you care for a snack?" It was the second time Roman had made himself scarce. He resurfaced again only a month later, as I recall. One and a half months to be precise, I said as I pulled down my tray table. One and a half months was all it took for Roman to finish reading all, or almost all the available books by Thomas Bernhard. At least that was the excuse he gave that evening. I did nothing but gorge myself on Thomas Bernhard, he said, in six weeks I left my house no more than four times, and the few times I did go out—which was hardly at all, since I've always preferred immobility to hyperactivity—were strictly limited to within the immediate surroundings of my small apartment. Just after ordering our traditional bottle of red in the downtown dive—the Babylon, I believe it was called—just after he had placed our order, I thought, Roman confirmed that he had read through almost all of Thomas Bernhard's novels back to back in the space of six weeks, and that Thomas Bernhard, more than any other, was most assuredly the writer who had ripped him off the most. More than Kafka, more than Beckett, more than anyone. Six weeks of seclusion and intensive reading and a total blackout with regard to the outside world were enough, said Roman, these six weeks were more than enough to convince me that Thomas Bernhard had not only charted the territory and foreclosed the language on me, crimes for which, it should be said, he has numerous co-conspirators, but also ripped off my ideas in full. Now that I have read and reread Thomas Bernhard for six straight weeks I can say without hesitation that in actual fact, Thomas Bernhard ripped off—start to finish—my ideas, my personal experience, and my aesthetic concerns. In their entirety. Whether they have to do with war and the forgetting that prolongs it and the effects of that war on the collective imagination; or with the inexhaustible hatred and ambivalence with regard to the native country; or the *metaphysical* impossibility of anything to start or finish anywhere but in death; or whether it's more generally about the *confinement of the mind* in a deadly cycle of mental repetition; yes, all these ideas and all these concerns, which I owe clearly to *my personal experience and my own imagination* have all been ripped off, *wholesale*, by Thomas Bernhard. Whether my ideas and my experiences are authentic or imagined, whether those of Thomas Bernhard are genuine or made up, in other words, the fact that these ideas are more or less consistent with any of our *personal* biographies, is of no importance, said Roman that evening, this is not all about the *veracity* of facts and opinions from either of us, nor is it even about a hypothetical identification with the various fictional characters of Thomas Bernhard, all that is absolutely beside the point, but it's the rip-off, the punishable offense of out and out robbery. I could open to any page of Thomas Bernhard and show you, with supporting evidence, so to speak, that this very page opened at random contains a shameless *display* of some idea of mine, two or three of my personal experiences and as many of my aesthetic obsessions. Completely by chance. On every page. All of this on display on every page completely by chance, said Roman. On display in *L'Origine*, on display in *Des arbres à abattre*, in *Béton*, in *Extinction*, and in all those that I read and reread. In each of these books there are *at the very least* one or two examples of highway robbery per page, at least one or two ripped-off ideas. Well obviously I was sick to my stomach, one or two to per page, I was literally sick to my stomach; and yet I couldn't stop myself. Not if I'd come this far, as they say. I wanted to know just how badly Thomas Bernhard was going to rip off my mind. How far he would go to rob me blind and *how far he had gone not to flatter me, but to actually silence and destroy me.* What I sensed from the moment I leafed through *L'Origine* is now fully realized, said Roman, downing his glass of red, at the end of these sickening readings and in an indescribable state of collapse, I understood that at the same time they deprived me of my ideas and my current experiences as a whole—an aggravation in itself appalling enough to bear repeating—Thomas Bernhard had lived, thought, and written down my life and my ideas in my place, and I realized that he had also and most especially compromised my chances of ever finding *something new* to think or say or write, if it ever came to that. Thomas Bernhard has indeed compromised my chances of ever finding something new to think and to say, that's the bottom line, he had *quite simply optioned all my future ideas,* Roman said, he had somehow essentially destroyed in advance all of my future thoughts and all of the projects that might one day materialize. Naturally, I must have somewhere in my possession some personal ideas still intact, said Roman while I refilled our glasses, in the midst of this huge undertaking of systematic looting, there must certainly be, let's say, two or three ideas left over—at the very least—that I managed to *conceal,* theoretically there ought to be something new left to think or say, but in the end this doesn't mean much, does it? These are only minor details. Probably residues of individuality. *Mere pittance.* "An hour and a half! We'll be there in a little over an hour and a half!" After all, I could have written all these novels myself, continued Roman after a slight pause, my *Béton,* my *Extinction,* or my *L'Origine*, sure, why not after all? That Thomas Bernhard managed to write them is proof in itself that my ideas and my obsessions and my experiences were quite valid, so I very well could have written my own *Maîtres anciens,* my own *Oui*, or my own *Gel* after all. Perhaps not in the immediate future but I still could have. I guess not before overcoming my inability to start or finish anything, but I still could have. You could even imagine that if, at some unspecified time in the future, I was inclined to sit down to write about *foregone conclusions*, I could have written all of these novels. Instead of which, I am from *now on*, either silenced or doomed to imitation. For now and forever the whole notion of *eventuality* has been taken away from me, by writing all of these novels full of my ideas Thomas Bernhard simply doomed me to silence or imitation, and *even though they are my own ideas* I can do no more than choose between two equally lifeless and grim perspectives: *silence or imitation*. Silence or duplication, to be precise. A more or less dull duplicate, a more or less nasty duplicate; but a duplicate all the same. Thinking and writing a new version of *L'Origine*, or a new version of *Gel*, or a new version of *Oui* in itself would involve no particular interest or major challenges, said Roman, to write my version of *L'Origine* or *Gel* or *Oui* I would only have to sit down and pull the wool over my eyes. It would cost me no more effort than to sit down, and then pretend that these three novels had never existed, and then accept that my *L'Origine* or my *Gel* or my *Oui* is ultimately only a copy. This would necessarily result in a copy said Roman, and this is within virtually everyone's means. Indeed nothing is more accessible to the mind than the implementation of schemes that another mind has developed before him and nothing is easier, more automatic, more natural to the mind than a copy—in short, *obedience.* A mind asks only to obey, and that's the truth, *to obey infinitely but in good conscience*, meaning with the impression of preserving its singularity while rebelling at every turn. "I'm just going to take one last trip to the john. I'll be right back." Instead of keeping my mind busy with *compositions* that had been my own—and that Thomas Bernhard totally ripped off—I find myself effectively silenced and reduced to imitation. And to an imitation all the more pathetically lame in that it will never reproduce, exactly and in the same terms, the object of its imitation. At best it would be my version of *Oui,* or my version of *Gel,* or my version of *L'Origine,* in other words, not a whole lot: *a kind of relatively pointless replica that won't cancel out the original, yet written with the loot of my own ideas.* At best, no matter how they turned out, they would be nothing more than faded, bland and frankly impoverished versions of the originals by Thomas Bernhard. So again, not a whole lot—the ravings of a maniac writer. Unless I were to copy out word for word *Oui,* or *Gel,* or *L'Origine* by Thomas Bernhard, unless I were to proceed the way Pierre Menard proceeded with Cervantes, unless I were to shed my last remaining residue of individuality, my good conscience, my vague attempts at originality—this "not a whole lot" that has turned out to be so hard to discard—I would not be able to duplicate the exact wording of Thomas Bernhard's originals. (During his six-week reclusion, I thought while making room one last time for the fidgety Biroult, Roman had read, at the same time as all available Thomas Bernhard books, he read "Pierre Menard, Author of the Quixote," a short story by Borges. Behind the obvious humor of Borges, Roman had found, in this short text of a dozen pages, the very essence of art, to quote his own terms. What Menard did with *Don Quixote* is an embodiment of the artistic ideal, he said later in the evening, an exceptional feat. In proposing a new version of *Don Quixote* that actually just reproduces every sentence of Cervantes word for word, *Pierre Menard not only shed his own persona, but also transformed himself completely into Cervantes*—he took a stand for freedom. To reproduce word for word what another has written, all without changing a single line, this very much outperforms the work of Cervantes himself, as *Cervantes only had to be Cervantes to write his Don Quixote.* Pierre Menard very simply delivered a *second original* of *Don Quixote* to the world: an exceptional feat, he repeated later in the evening, without a doubt one of the great achievements of the mind.) As long as my eventual versions and my eventual copies, all necessarily altered unless I renounce the last residue of my individuality, as long as they still *resemble me a little too much*, it will be impossible to deliver anything other than an *equivalent* of the novels of Thomas Bernhard, a kind of fakery, so to speak, whereas the precise objective is to replicate the novels of Thomas Bernhard, to exactly reproduce the novels of Thomas Bernhard. Strictly speaking there is no such thing as forgery of literary masterpieces, that privilege being reserved exclusively to painting, said Roman, in literature there are only equivalents, closet copies, and superfluous versions that, to make things worse, will never erase the slightest trace of the original, it's their manufacturer's defect, so to speak. Unless you have Pierre Menard's genius, which has succeeded so masterfully at erasing all traces of the original *Don Quixote* by flinging another original *Don Quixote* at us, it's useless to dream of a more glorious fate than that of a virtuoso copycat. And for my part, since I will never be able to create a *perfect duplicate* of the novels of Thomas Bernhard I am doomed, indefinitely and without further ado, to the infamous status of a virtuoso copycat, meaning, basically, someone very obedient. In the best case scenario, I could never hope for anything better than the dubious fate of a virtuoso—*like everyone else*—and that's the bottom line. *Like everyone else.* But I still have the option of *silence*, Roman hastened to add the evening of our last meeting, so I have nothing more to say. While nonchalantly making room for good old Biroult one last time, who since his long stay in the john is now looking like a new man, probably in connection with the generous layer of Italian pomade that he slathered all over his hair, and who seems to be more and more excited at the prospect of visiting a country whose past, present, and future horrors he obviously hasn't a clue about, it occurred to me that our evening at the Babylon bar was actually my last evening with

Roman, and that his "I have nothing more to say" was the last, the very last sentence he addressed to me. He rose, crumpled his empty cigarette pack, disappeared into the gloom of the Babylon, and that was that. Besides, what more could he have added? How could you say anything more after such a confession? Such evidence of lucidity. Or self-contempt. Naturally, not a word from him since, *blackout* from both sides. On purpose. Since that last night I deliberately cut off all contact and, in a more general way, strictly refrained from even thinking about him. I was utterly determined to block out that whole chunk of my life, to wipe the slate clean, as they say. Even his old notebook, which he gave me as a keepsake—I am now convinced of it—on that evening at the Babylon, because by then he believed he had already been consigned to the destiny he so feared, the virtuoso, even that old notebook that I'm coming to return to him in person, I have never really taken a good look at. Too many things still remind me of him, get mixed up in my head, so that I couldn't ever really afford to, I thought to myself, in a state of exhaustion beyond telling. The past, the country, the language, Roman still embodies them all and will continue to for a very long time to come, whether he knows it or not. Impossible to disentangle them. No matter what I do, it's impossible to disentangle them. A moment of inattention or carelessness, or some little nostalgic thought, and it's all the past and the country and the language that rears its ugly head, a tiny innocent thought, and it's Roman's voice that takes the place of mine and all of Roman's questions that take the place of mine and all of Roman takes my place and I can't afford that, no I simply can't afford that because I'm just not Roman and because I'm not the same anymore and it's this trip, I thought, softly folding my synthetic blanket, it's this damn trip. And with that, I slept, I slept the sleep of the dead.

OLIVER ROHE was born in 1972 to a German father and an Armenian mother from Lebanon. He is a novelist and critic, and a founding member of the literary review *Inculte.* His novel *Vacant Lot* was published in an English translation by Laird Hunt in 2010.

LAUREN MESSINA is a freelance translator based in Illinois.

JANE KUNTZ has translated, among other titles, *Hotel Crystal* by Olivier Rolin, *Pigeon Post* by Dumitru Tsepeneag, and *Hoppla! 1 2 3* by Gérard Gavarry, all of which are available from Dalkey Archive Press.

## SELECTED DALKEY ARCHIVE TITLES

Michal Ajvaz, *The Golden Age.*
*The Other City.*
Pierre Albert-Birot, *Grabinoulor.*
Yuz Aleshkovsky, *Kangaroo.*
Felipe Alfau, *Chromos.*
*Locos.*
Ivan Ângelo, *The Celebration.*
*The Tower of Glass.*
António Lobo Antunes, *Knowledge of Hell.*
*The Splendor of Portugal.*
Alain Arias-Misson, *Theatre of Incest.*
John Ashbery and James Schuyler, *A Nest of Ninnies.*
Robert Ashley, *Perfect Lives.*
Gabriela Avigur-Rotem, *Heatwave and Crazy Birds.*
Djuna Barnes, *Ladies Almanack.*
*Ryder.*
John Barth, *LETTERS.*
*Sabbatical.*
Donald Barthelme, *The King.*
*Paradise.*
Svetislav Basara, *Chinese Letter.*
Miquel Bauçà, *The Siege in the Room.*
René Belletto, *Dying.*
Marek Bieńczyk, *Transparency.*
Andrei Bitov, *Pushkin House.*
Andrej Blatnik, *You Do Understand.*
Louis Paul Boon, *Chapel Road.*
*My Little War.*
*Summer in Termuren.*
Roger Boylan, *Killoyle.*
Ignácio de Loyola Brandão, *Anonymous Celebrity.*
*Zero.*
Bonnie Bremser, *Troia: Mexican Memoirs.*
Christine Brooke-Rose, *Amalgamemnon.*
Brigid Brophy, *In Transit.*
Gerald L. Bruns, *Modern Poetry and the Idea of Language.*
Gabrielle Burton, *Heartbreak Hotel.*
Michel Butor, *Degrees.*
*Mobile.*
G. Cabrera Infante, *Infante's Inferno.*
*Three Trapped Tigers.*
Julieta Campos, *The Fear of Losing Eurydice.*
Anne Carson, *Eros the Bittersweet.*
Orly Castel-Bloom, *Dolly City.*
Louis-Ferdinand Céline, *Castle to Castle.*
*Conversations with Professor Y.*
*London Bridge.*
*Normance.*
*North.*
*Rigadoon.*
Marie Chaix, *The Laurels of Lake Constance.*
Hugo Charteris, *The Tide Is Right.*
Eric Chevillard, *Demolishing Nisard.*
Marc Cholodenko, *Mordechai Schamz.*
Joshua Cohen, *Witz.*
Emily Holmes Coleman, *The Shutter of Snow.*
Robert Coover, *A Night at the Movies.*
Stanley Crawford, *Log of the S.S. The Mrs Unguentine.*
*Some Instructions to My Wife.*
René Crevel, *Putting My Foot in It.*
Ralph Cusack, *Cadenza.*
Nicholas Delbanco, *The Count of Concord.*
*Sherbrookes.*
Nigel Dennis, *Cards of Identity.*
Peter Dimock, *A Short Rhetoric for Leaving the Family.*
Ariel Dorfman, *Konfidenz.*
Coleman Dowell,
*Island People.*
*Too Much Flesh and Jabez.*
Arkadii Dragomoshchenko, *Dust.*
Rikki Ducornet, *The Complete Butcher's Tales.*
*The Fountains of Neptune.*
*The Jade Cabinet.*
*Phosphor in Dreamland.*
William Eastlake, *The Bamboo Bed.*
*Castle Keep.*
*Lyric of the Circle Heart.*
Jean Echenoz, *Chopin's Move.*
Stanley Elkin, *A Bad Man.*
*Criers and Kibitzers, Kibitzers and Criers.*
*The Dick Gibson Show.*
*The Franchiser.*
*The Living End.*
*Mrs. Ted Bliss.*
François Emmanuel, *Invitation to a Voyage.*
Salvador Espriu, *Ariadne in the Grotesque Labyrinth.*
Leslie A. Fiedler, *Love and Death in the American Novel.*
Juan Filloy, *Op Oloop.*
Andy Fitch, *Pop Poetics.*
Gustave Flaubert, *Bouvard and Pécuchet.*
Kass Fleisher, *Talking out of School.*
Ford Madox Ford,
*The March of Literature.*
Jon Fosse, *Aliss at the Fire.*
*Melancholy.*
Max Frisch, *I'm Not Stiller.*
*Man in the Holocene.*
Carlos Fuentes, *Christopher Unborn.*
*Distant Relations.*
*Terra Nostra.*
*Where the Air Is Clear.*
Takehiko Fukunaga, *Flowers of Grass.*
William Gaddis, *J R.*
*The Recognitions.*
Janice Galloway, *Foreign Parts.*
*The Trick Is to Keep Breathing.*
William H. Gass, *Cartesian Sonata and Other Novellas.*
*Finding a Form.*
*A Temple of Texts.*
*The Tunnel.*
*Willie Masters' Lonesome Wife.*
Gérard Gavarry, *Hoppla! 1 2 3.*
Etienne Gilson,
*The Arts of the Beautiful.*
*Forms and Substances in the Arts.*
C. S. Giscombe, *Giscome Road.*
*Here.*
Douglas Glover, *Bad News of the Heart.*
Witold Gombrowicz,
*A Kind of Testament.*
Paulo Emílio Sales Gomes, *P's Three Women.*
Georgi Gospodinov, *Natural Novel.*
Juan Goytisolo, *Count Julian.*
*Juan the Landless.*
*Makbara.*
*Marks of Identity.*

## SELECTED DALKEY ARCHIVE TITLES

Henry Green, *Back.*
*Blindness.*
*Concluding.*
*Doting.*
*Nothing.*
Jack Green, *Fire the Bastards!*
Jiří Gruša, *The Questionnaire.*
Mela Hartwig, *Am I a Redundant Human Being?*
John Hawkes, *The Passion Artist.*
*Whistlejacket.*
Elizabeth Heighway, ed., *Contemporary Georgian Fiction.*
Aleksandar Hemon, ed., *Best European Fiction.*
Aidan Higgins, *Balcony of Europe.*
*Blind Man's Bluff*
*Bornholm Night-Ferry.*
*Flotsam and Jetsam.*
*Langrishe, Go Down.*
*Scenes from a Receding Past.*
Keizo Hino, *Isle of Dreams.*
Kazushi Hosaka, *Plainsong.*
Aldous Huxley, *Antic Hay.*
*Crome Yellow.*
*Point Counter Point.*
*Those Barren Leaves.*
*Time Must Have a Stop.*
Naoyuki Ii, *The Shadow of a Blue Cat.*
Gert Jonke, *The Distant Sound.*
*Geometric Regional Novel.*
*Homage to Czerny.*
*The System of Vienna.*
Jacques Jouet, *Mountain R.*
*Savage.*
*Upstaged.*
Mieko Kanai, *The Word Book.*
Yoram Kaniuk, *Life on Sandpaper.*
Hugh Kenner, *Flaubert.*
*Joyce and Beckett: The Stoic Comedians.*
*Joyce's Voices.*
Danilo Kiš, *The Attic.*
*Garden, Ashes.*
*The Lute and the Scars*
*Psalm 44.*
*A Tomb for Boris Davidovich.*
Anita Konkka, *A Fool's Paradise.*
George Konrád, *The City Builder.*
Tadeusz Konwicki, *A Minor Apocalypse.*
*The Polish Complex.*
Menis Koumandareas, *Koula.*
Elaine Kraf, *The Princess of 72nd Street.*
Jim Krusoe, *Iceland.*
Ayşe Kulin, *Farewell: A Mansion in Occupied Istanbul.*
Emilio Lascano Tegui, *On Elegance While Sleeping.*
Eric Laurrent, *Do Not Touch.*
Violette Leduc, *La Bâtarde.*
Edouard Levé, *Autoportrait.*
*Suicide.*
Mario Levi, *Istanbul Was a Fairy Tale.*
Deborah Levy, *Billy and Girl.*
José Lezama Lima, *Paradiso.*
Rosa Liksom, *Dark Paradise.*
Osman Lins, *Avalovara.*
*The Queen of the Prisons of Greece.*
Alf Mac Lochlainn,
*The Corpus in the Library.*
*Out of Focus.*
Ron Loewinsohn, *Magnetic Field(s).*
Mina Loy, *Stories and Essays of Mina Loy.*
D. Keith Mano, *Take Five.*
Micheline Aharonian Marcom,
*The Mirror in the Well.*
Ben Marcus,
*The Age of Wire and String.*
Wallace Markfield,
*Teitlebaum's Window.*
*To an Early Grave.*
David Markson, *Reader's Block.*
*Wittgenstein's Mistress.*
Carole Maso, *AVA.*
Ladislav Matejka and Krystyna Pomorska, eds.,
*Readings in Russian Poetics: Formalist and Structuralist Views.*
Harry Mathews, *Cigarettes.*
*The Conversions.*
*The Human Country: New and Collected Stories.*
*The Journalist.*
*My Life in CIA.*
*Singular Pleasures.*
*The Sinking of the Odradek Stadium.*
*Tlooth.*
Joseph McElroy,
*Night Soul and Other Stories.*
Abdelwahab Meddeb, *Talismano.*
Gerhard Meier, *Isle of the Dead.*
Herman Melville, *The Confidence-Man.*
Amanda Michalopoulou, *I'd Like.*
Steven Millhauser, *The Barnum Museum.*
*In the Penny Arcade.*
Ralph J. Mills, Jr., *Essays on Poetry.*
Momus, *The Book of Jokes.*
Christine Montalbetti, *The Origin of Man.*
*Western.*
Olive Moore, *Spleen.*
Nicholas Mosley, *Accident.*
*Assassins.*
*Catastrophe Practice.*
*Experience and Religion.*
*A Garden of Trees.*
*Hopeful Monsters.*
*Imago Bird.*
*Impossible Object.*
*Inventing God.*
*Judith.*
*Look at the Dark.*
*Natalie Natalia.*
*Serpent.*
*Time at War.*
Warren Motte,
*Fables of the Novel: French Fiction since 1990.*
*Fiction Now: The French Novel in the 21st Century.*
*Oulipo: A Primer of Potential Literature.*
Gerald Murnane, *Barley Patch.*
*Inland.*
Yves Navarre, *Our Share of Time.*
*Sweet Tooth.*
Dorothy Nelson, *In Night's City.*
*Tar and Feathers.*
Eshkol Nevo, *Homesick.*
Wilfrido D. Nolledo, *But for the Lovers.*
Flann O'Brien, *At Swim-Two-Birds.*
*The Best of Myles.*
*The Dalkey Archive.*
*The Hard Life.*
*The Poor Mouth.*

## SELECTED DALKEY ARCHIVE TITLES

The Third Policeman.
CLAUDE OLLIER, *The Mise-en-Scène.*
*Wert and the Life Without End.*
GIOVANNI ORELLI, *Walaschek's Dream.*
PATRIK OUŘEDNÍK, *Europeana.*
*The Opportune Moment, 1855.*
BORIS PAHOR, *Necropolis.*
FERNANDO DEL PASO, *News from the Empire.*
*Palinuro of Mexico.*
ROBERT PINGET, *The Inquisitory.*
*Mahu or The Material.*
*Trio.*
MANUEL PUIG, *Betrayed by Rita Hayworth.*
*The Buenos Aires Affair.*
*Heartbreak Tango.*
RAYMOND QUENEAU, *The Last Days.*
*Odile.*
*Pierrot Mon Ami.*
*Saint Glinglin.*
ANN QUIN, *Berg.*
*Passages.*
*Three.*
*Tripticks.*
ISHMAEL REED, *The Free-Lance Pallbearers.*
*The Last Days of Louisiana Red.*
*Ishmael Reed: The Plays.*
*Juice!*
*Reckless Eyeballing.*
*The Terrible Threes.*
*The Terrible Twos.*
*Yellow Back Radio Broke-Down.*
JASIA REICHARDT, *15 Journeys Warsaw to London.*
NOËLLE REVAZ, *With the Animals.*
JOÃO UBALDO RIBEIRO, *House of the Fortunate Buddhas.*
JEAN RICARDOU, *Place Names.*
RAINER MARIA RILKE, *The Notebooks of Malte Laurids Brigge.*
JULIÁN RÍOS, *The House of Ulysses.*
*Larva: A Midsummer Night's Babel.*
*Poundemonium.*
*Procession of Shadows.*
AUGUSTO ROA BASTOS, *I the Supreme.*
DANIËL ROBBERECHTS, *Arriving in Avignon.*
JEAN ROLIN, *The Explosion of the Radiator Hose.*
OLIVIER ROLIN, *Hotel Crystal.*
ALIX CLEO ROUBAUD, *Alix's Journal.*
JACQUES ROUBAUD, *The Form of a City Changes Faster, Alas, Than the Human Heart.*
*The Great Fire of London.*
*Hortense in Exile.*
*Hortense Is Abducted.*
*The Loop.*
*Mathematics:*
*The Plurality of Worlds of Lewis.*
*The Princess Hoppy.*
*Some Thing Black.*
RAYMOND ROUSSEL, *Impressions of Africa.*
VEDRANA RUDAN, *Night.*
STIG SÆTERBAKKEN, *Siamese.*
*Self Control.*
LYDIE SALVAYRE, *The Company of Ghosts.*
*The Lecture.*
*The Power of Flies.*
LUIS RAFAEL SÁNCHEZ, *Macho Camacho's Beat.*
SEVERO SARDUY, *Cobra & Maitreya.*
NATHALIE SARRAUTE, *Do You Hear Them?*
*Martereau.*
*The Planetarium.*
ARNO SCHMIDT, *Collected Novellas.*
*Collected Stories.*
*Nobodaddy's Children.*
*Two Novels.*
ASAF SCHURR, *Motti.*
GAIL SCOTT, *My Paris.*
DAMION SEARLS, *What We Were Doing and Where We Were Going.*
JUNE AKERS SEESE, *Is This What Other Women Feel Too?*
*What Waiting Really Means.*
BERNARD SHARE, *Inish.*
*Transit.*
VIKTOR SHKLOVSKY, *Bowstring.*
*Knight's Move.*
*A Sentimental Journey: Memoirs 1917–1922.*
*Energy of Delusion: A Book on Plot.*
*Literature and Cinematography.*
*Theory of Prose.*
*Third Factory.*
*Zoo, or Letters Not about Love.*
PIERRE SINIAC, *The Collaborators.*
KJERSTI A. SKOMSVOLD, *The Faster I Walk, the Smaller I Am.*
JOSEF ŠKVORECKÝ, *The Engineer of Human Souls.*
GILBERT SORRENTINO, *Aberration of Starlight.*
*Blue Pastoral.*
*Crystal Vision.*
*Imaginative Qualities of Actual Things.*
*Mulligan Stew.*
*Pack of Lies.*
*Red the Fiend.*
*The Sky Changes.*
*Something Said.*
*Splendide-Hôtel.*
*Steelwork.*
*Under the Shadow.*
W. M. SPACKMAN, *The Complete Fiction.*
ANDRZEJ STASIUK, *Dukla.*
*Fado.*
GERTRUDE STEIN, *The Making of Americans.*
*A Novel of Thank You.*
LARS SVENDSEN, *A Philosophy of Evil.*
PIOTR SZEWC, *Annihilation.*
GONÇALO M. TAVARES, *Jerusalem.*
*Joseph Walser's Machine.*
*Learning to Pray in the Age of Technique.*
LUCIAN DAN TEODOROVICI, *Our Circus Presents . . .*
NIKANOR TERATOLOGEN, *Assisted Living.*
STEFAN THEMERSON, *Hobson's Island.*
*The Mystery of the Sardine.*
*Tom Harris.*
TAEKO TOMIOKA, *Building Waves.*
JOHN TOOMEY, *Sleepwalker.*
JEAN-PHILIPPE TOUSSAINT, *The Bathroom.*
*Camera.*
*Monsieur.*
*Reticence.*
*Running Away.*
*Self-Portrait Abroad.*
*Television.*
*The Truth about Marie.*

## SELECTED DALKEY ARCHIVE TITLES

Dumitru Tsepeneag, *Hotel Europa.*
*The Necessary Marriage.*
*Pigeon Post.*
*Vain Art of the Fugue.*
Esther Tusquets, *Stranded.*
Dubravka Ugresic, *Lend Me Your Character.*
*Thank You for Not Reading.*
Tor Ulven, *Replacement.*
Mati Unt, *Brecht at Night.*
*Diary of a Blood Donor.*
*Things in the Night.*
Álvaro Uribe and Olivia Sears, eds., *Best of Contemporary Mexican Fiction.*
Eloy Urroz, *Friction.*
*The Obstacles.*
Luisa Valenzuela, *Dark Desires and the Others.*
*He Who Searches.*
Paul Verhaeghen, *Omega Minor.*
Aglaja Veteranyi, *Why the Child Is Cooking in the Polenta.*
Boris Vian, *Heartsnatcher.*
Llorenç Villalonga, *The Dolls' Room.*
Toomas Vint, *An Unending Landscape.*
Ornela Vorpsi, *The Country Where No One Ever Dies.*
Austryn Wainhouse, *Hedyphagetica.*
Curtis White, *America's Magic Mountain.*
*The Idea of Home.*
*Memories of My Father Watching TV.*
*Requiem.*
Diane Williams, *Excitability: Selected Stories.*
*Romancer Erector.*
Douglas Woolf, *Wall to Wall.*
*Ya! & John-Juan.*
Jay Wright, *Polynomials and Pollen.*
*The Presentable Art of Reading Absence.*
Philip Wylie, *Generation of Vipers.*
Marguerite Young, *Angel in the Forest.*
*Miss MacIntosh, My Darling.*
Reyoung, *Unbabbling.*
Vlado Žabot, *The Succubus.*
Zoran Živković, *Hidden Camera.*
Louis Zukofsky, *Collected Fiction.*
Vitomil Zupan, *Minuet for Guitar.*
Scott Zwiren, *God Head.*